The Swords of Unforgotten Memories

Secrets Beneath the Ripples

Sheena O'Loughlin

Wordspree Books

Published in Ireland by Wordspree Books in 2023
ISBN 978-1-7384228-1-4

Sheena O'Loughlin asserts the moral right to be identified as the author of this work.

This novel is entirely a work of fiction.

The names, characters, places, and incidents portrayed in it are the work of the author's imagination. Any resemblance to the actual living persons, living or dead, events or localities is purely entirely coincidental.

Book cover designed by Md Ratul IR

About the Author

Sheena O'Loughlin, an Irish author who works as an accountant, writes with a clear dream: to create her own short indie horror game. It's this very aspiration that drew her into the world of storytelling. Outside of her professional life, Sheena unwinds with TV shows, video games, refreshing walks, and quality time with friends and family.

Stay connected with Sheena's journey:

Facebook: https://www.facebook.com/sheens987
Twitter/X: www.x.com/sheens987
Instagram: https://Instagram.com/sheens987
Ream: https://reamstories.com/profile/ln7i65c6x0

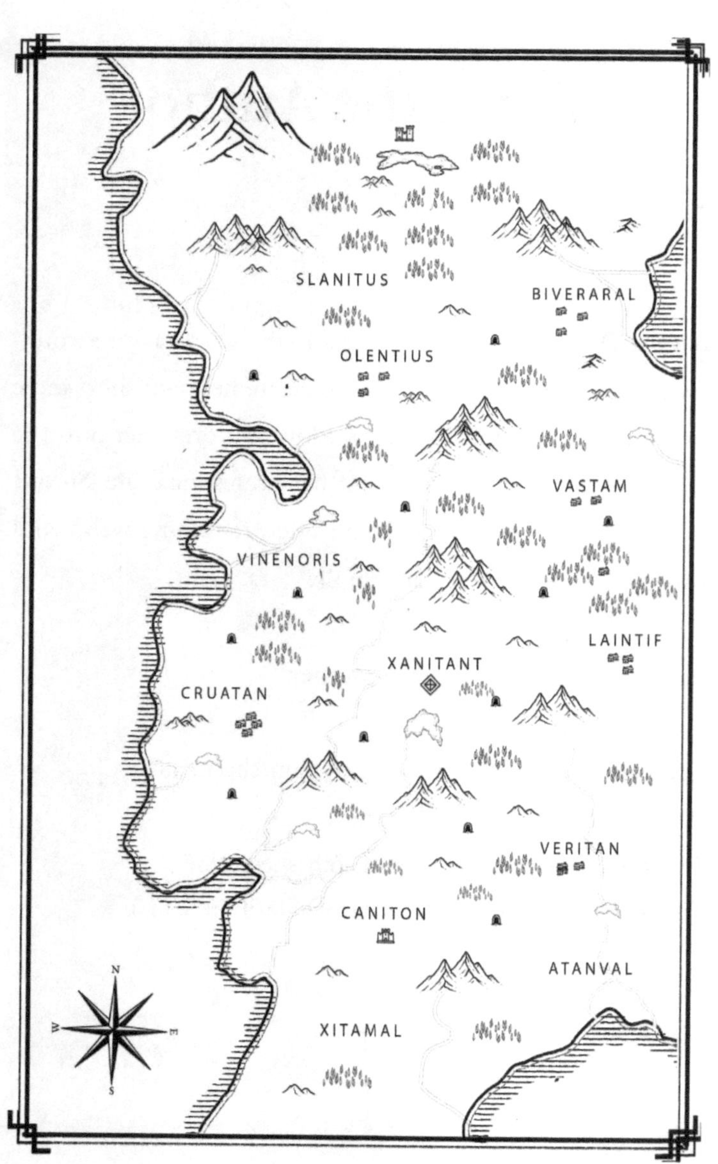

SLANITUS
BIVERARAL
OLENTIUS
VASTAM
VINENORIS
LAINTIF
XANITANT
CRUATAN
VERITAN
CANITON
ATANVAL
XITAMAL
N
S
W
E

Contents

Chapter One
Mysterious Forest

The young girl's screams pierced through the wind.

The note of terror hung in the dense night air, jolting a sudden surge of fear through The Stranger.

The Stranger spun his head towards the sound, his eyes narrowed as he assessed the situation.

With a sharp whistle, The Stranger summoned his horse and sprang onto its back, urging the animal into a furious gallop through the treacherous forest.

The Stranger's heart pounded with adrenaline as he pushed the horse to its limits.

The ominous trees loomed overhead, casting eerie shadows.

But The Stranger was undaunted as he drew closer to the noise.

The Stranger's stomach churned when he spotted a young girl cornered by an eerie, growling Wolagist in the distance.

This fearsome fusion of wolf and dragon had the body of a massive wolf and the wings and tail of a dragon, with razor-sharp teeth and claws capable of tearing through even the sturdiest of armour.

Its fur was a sharp red, barely visible in the darkness, and its piercing blue eyes glinted towards the young girl's screams.

As The Stranger urged his horse to go faster, he found himself between the Wolagist and the young girl.

The Stranger leapt from his horse, whipping out his sword and circling the dragon-wolf hybrid.

With laser-like focus, the Wolagist turned its attention to The Stranger, baring its teeth and emitting a piercing howl that made The Stranger crumble to the mossy ground, cupping his hands over his ears in agony.

The Wolagist charged at lightning speed, knocking The Stranger to the ground, and crawled on top of him, piercing its talons into The Stranger's torso.

The Stranger screamed in pain through his clenched teeth, desperately trying to reach his sword, which was just out of reach.

The Stranger closed his eyes and focused.

As the Wolagist lifted its talons from his torso, The Stranger instinctively rolled to his side, getting scratched across his chest as he swiftly picked up his sword and stabbed the Wolagist, causing it to emit a final, piercing howl before falling to the ground.

The Stranger collapsed to the ground, his chest heaving as he struggled to catch his breath.

After a moment, The Stranger lifted himself and stumbled towards the young girl.

Her thin, wavy brown hair covered her face as she sobbed uncontrollably.

The Stranger carefully picked her up, placing her chest on his left side to avoid aggravating his wounds.

Holding her close, The Stranger whispered, "You're safe now, and I promise I will bring you home."

The Stranger whistled for his horse, which rushed to his side.

The Stranger gently lifted the young girl onto the horse and mounted it behind her, holding her tightly as he urged the horse to move.

As they rode swiftly through the gloomy forest, The Stranger could sense the tension in the air.

The Stranger felt a growing unease as he sensed swift movement and heard distant howls echoing through the trees.

A pack of wolves rushed past them, ignoring them as they disappeared deeper into the forest.

The Stranger breathed a sigh of relief, grateful that the pack had not seen them as potential prey.

But his relief was short-lived as a loud, thunderous roar echoed through the forest, and the pained cries of the wolves followed it.

The Stranger's body froze briefly as a chilling sensation slithered down his back, and he urged his horse to move faster.

They rode towards the village of Vinenoris with renewed urgency, knowing that dangers could still lurk around every corner in this dark and foreboding forest.

As they rode, The Stranger couldn't help but wonder what kind of creature had caused the roar that had silenced the pack of wolves.

The Stranger knew they needed to be on their guard, for there was no telling what other dangers may lie ahead.

The Stranger led his horse and the young girl into the quaint outskirts of Vinenoris.

The rhythmic echo of their steeds' hooves reverberated through the narrow cobblestone paths that wound their way through the village.

The feeble glow of flickering flames from scattered torches illuminated the path, revealing huddled thatched-roof cottages.

The Stranger's eyes scanned the area for the girl's parents.

A piercing wail tore through The Stranger's ears, causing the young girl to cry in distress.

The young girl's tiny frame trembled as she struggled to dismount from the horse, her tearful pleas for her mother echoing through the chaos.

The Stranger swiftly turned to the noise source and gently lifted the young girl, easing her down to the cobblestone ground.

The girl sprinted towards her mother, who embraced her tightly and glared suspiciously at The Stranger.

The Stranger, anticipating her reaction, spoke in a deep, throaty voice, "I saved her from a Wolagist, a deadly creature that would have killed her if I hadn't intervened. I killed the Wolagist, but the forest is unsafe for anyone, let alone a young girl."

The mother gasped in horror.

She spoke faster, "My apologies, Sir; how can I repay you? I don't have much to give, but..."

The Stranger moved closer to her, the village fire flames giving light and revealing his pale face and tangled, wavy brown hair falling down his face.

The Stranger's piercing brown eyes relaxed as he approached the lady.

"All I need is for you to take care of my wounds, and I will be on my way," The Stranger said calmly.

The lady nodded and picked up her child, guiding The Stranger to her cottage.

Inside, the lady invited him to sit in the main room.

The Stranger's boots echoed off the chilled concrete floor as he sat on the stool beside the open fireplace.

The Stranger turned and stared deeply into the flames that flickered in a restless dance, conjuring images of a furious battle between men and monsters.

The Stranger drew in a deep breath, filling his lungs with the sharp, primal aroma of the burning wood, holding his wounds as he patiently waited for the woman's return.

The lady disappeared into a nearby bedroom.

After a moment, she reappeared, moving with deliberate steps towards The Stranger's side.

She paused, her voice lowered to a hushed tone. "Apologies, Sir, may I?"

The Stranger felt a gentle touch on his gambeson sleeve and nodded as the woman gently lifted the dark gambeson and tunic over his head, revealing his chest bloody with this fresh wound and a few old scars along his chest.

The woman hesitated momentarily, taking in the severity of the wounds, before composing herself to clean them, causing The Stranger to wince in pain.

"Sir, please come to this room and rest for the night to allow your wounds to heal," the woman said, motioning towards a bedroom on the far right.

The Stranger stood up and strolled towards the room.

As he followed the woman, she asked, "Sir, I hope you don't mind me asking, but what do you do for a living?"

The Stranger responded quietly, "I am just a nomad, nothing more."

"I hope you won't find it intrusive, but would you be willing to venture into the forest and protect us from the dangerous creatures that lurk within? We will compensate you with the coins gathered by the villagers. It should be sufficient," the woman asked hopefully.

She continued, "Once, we had guards from the kingdom of Xanitant who protected us in exchange for our crops. However, unfavourable weather has made it increasingly challenging to produce enough food for our people, let alone meet the kingdom's demands. To make matters worse, the greedy king of Xanitant now demands payment for guard services, leaving our village defenceless against the sinister creatures that roam the forest."

With pleading eyes, she beseeched The Stranger, "So, can you please help our village?"

The Stranger's head lowered, a sigh escaping softly, "Yes, madam. Tomorrow, I will venture into the forest and drive away any creatures I encounter. However, I must inform you that I must continue my way after tomorrow. I have obligations that await me. In return for my assistance, I merely request supplies to sustain me on my journey."

The woman nodded, directing The Stranger to rest in the bedroom.

In the morning, The Stranger left the cottage and walked to his horse, putting the supplies he had received from the woman in his horse's saddlebag.

The Stranger mounted the horse and travelled into the forest in search of any deadly creatures that lay within.

Chapter Two
Cruatan

Golden rays of dawn slipped past the lingering cloud cover, igniting the frost-rimmed winter morning with a welcome warmth.

A father and his young son walked up a winding path that led to a hill overlooking a breathtaking cliffside.

The air was crisp and filled with the scent of wildflowers as the father led the way with his rugged boots pressed against the earth, leaving imprints behind him.

Beside him, his son took hesitant steps, his eyes wide with wonderment.

Determinedly, they ascended the hill and approached the imposing statue, representing the most feared predator in Cruatanian lore.

The statue depicted the creature standing on its hind legs, its formidable height rivalling that of a dragon.

It was a masterful portrayal of a lean, muscular physique. Its coat, cast in solid stone, was as dark as the night sky, and its eyes were a captivating blend of black and yellow.

Opedius, the father, turned to his son, his brown eyes softening with warmth.

Opedius started their conversation in a voice as gentle as it was profound.

"Do you remember the tale about our ancestors and the great battle between the monsters and our people?"

His son's voice quivered slightly as he replied, "No, father. Is this why you brought me here?"

Opedius replied, "Yes, my son, it is vital that you listen."

Opedius turned away, striding toward the hill's edge, gazing down upon the village of Cruatan.

Below them, the rhythmic whisper of waves caressed the jagged cliffside, infusing the salty scent of the sea throughout the air of Cruatan.

Nestled near a dense forest, quaint cottages were scattered throughout the village.

The fourteen-year-old boy, Loac, scampered over to his father's side, looking up at the figure towering above him.

Opedius was robust, wearing a slightly wrinkled white jerkin rolled up to his elbows, revealing arms decorated with grime and scratches.

Opedius began his tale softly, "You see, Cruatan was not always the safe village, you know. The surrounding forest was home to the Egalait, a fearsome hybrid of eagle and alligator, that claimed many of our people's lives."

Loac fell silent, his eyes wide as he stared at his father.

Opedius continued, his gaze fixed on the village.

"Legends say that our goddess, Ferlenius, the goddess of fire and light, appeared to our ancestors during an annual ritual. In the fire pit's flames, she showed them a vision of our people under attack from these monsters alongside wooden statues of the most feared predator, Scanlist. This vision inspired our ancestors to create what you see behind us."

Loac glanced at the Scanlist statue and then turned his gaze back to his father, his mouth slightly open.

Opedius continued, "They crafted a horn that could mimic the terrifying roar of the Scanlist. Each night, the villagers smeared themselves in mud and blood, carrying the wooden Scanlist into the forest, blaring their horns and standing their ground against the predators. They continued this every night until the monsters fled our village for good."

Opedius sighed, looking at his son.

"The reason I'm telling you this is because I fear the forest is becoming dangerous again. A young girl was almost killed near Vinenoris, our neighbouring village to the north, just last night, but thankfully, a mysterious stranger saved her life. We need to leave this village soon. I am working on a safe plan to avoid encountering those beasts."

Opedius paused momentarily, then crouched to Loac's height, holding his son by the shoulders.

"Loac, I want us to go tracking later today. I know we've done it many times, but I need to know that if we ever get separated, you will always be able to find your way back to us. Can we please do it one last time?"

Loac stared at his father, then nodded, his voice firm. "Yes, I will, Father. I promise! And this time, I'll try my best."

Opedius, still maintaining eye contact, stood up.

His eyes were brimming with tears. "You're a good boy, Loac. We should head back home; your mother will be worried."

Heavy with emotion, they gradually descended the hill, heading home.

CHAPTER THREE
The Stranger

Loac splashed water onto his face, staring into the aged mirror hanging from a wall scarred by cracks and peeling paint.

Loac's mind was working overtime, conjuring up vivid images of the Egalait emerging from the forest's shadows and wreaking havoc throughout the village.

With a shiver, Loac forcefully shook off the threatening visions, letting reality seep back into his senses.

Splashing water onto his face again, Loac refocused on his reflection.

Loac's skin was as pale as an artist's untouched canvas, and had dark brown hair.

Loac sighed at his reflection and exited the dimly lit bathroom.

The rough timber floor creaked under his weight, the sound echoing through the silence in the cottage as he entered the living area to find Loac's parents seated at a wobbly wooden table, their chairs creaking under strain.

They looked up as Loac entered.

Loac found himself caught in the gaze of his mother, Brigid.

Brigid's blue eyes sparkled as she looked at him, and her long, soft brown hair cascaded down her back like a shimmering waterfall.

Brigid wore a plain cotton dress and tattered shoes she had carefully kept as clean as possible.

A fleeting smile graced Brigid's lips when her eyes met Loac's eyes, and then she scooted over to make room for Loac to sit between her and his father, Opedius.

Loac's approach was hesitant, the tension evident in his rigid posture.

Loac's gaze was fixed on his father, who sat silently, his focus consumed by the worn wooden table before him.

The room was as quiet as a hushed forest, the silence laced only by the scratching of Loac's stool as he took his place.

"What's wrong?" Loac asked, his voice trembling slightly with concern.

Opedius finally lifted his gaze, meeting Loac's eyes with a sombre expression.

Opedius's voice was soft yet firm when he responded, "Two young children ventured into the forest last night and haven't been seen since. We don't know if they're lost or if something happened to them. Loac, please, promise me you won't go into the forest. It's not safe anymore."

Loac, still as a statue, nodded in agreement, his gaze still fixed on his father's troubled expression.

Opedius continued, his voice barely above a whisper.

"I still plan to go tracking with you today, but could you please feed and walk the dogs for now? I would walk them myself, but I have something to do."

Without hesitation, Loac sprung from his seat.

Loac reached for the dog food and headed to care for his furry companions.

"Cathal! Finn!" Loac hollered after whistling.

"Come here, boys."

Cathal, the cheerful golden retriever, rushed out first.

His bum wriggled excessively in anticipation of food.

Finn, the Husky, trotted over and did his usual dance, lifting his front paws up and down while he impatiently waited for Loac to put the food dish down.

Once the dogs finished eating, Loac opened the gate, and the dogs rushed out but stopped, glancing back at Loac.

As Loac walked into the street of Cruatan, the sun crept over the horizon.

The village came to life with the bustle of daily chores. The town was a cluster of thatched cottages constructed of wattle and daub.

Narrow cobblestone paths led to the outskirts, where more prominent barley and wheat fields swayed in the gentle morning breeze.

Loac tied Cathal and Finn's leashes to the wooden gate outside the bakery before walking in to get some bread.

Once Loac reemerged from the bakery, he caught sight of a man shrouded in a dark hood, a long black cloak, and black boots on his feet.

The Stranger was wearing a lightly armoured suit and had a sword resting by his side.

Loac's focus was captivated by the sword's hilt, which featured an intricate arrangement of objects, including a gnomon from a sundial, a paintbrush top, and various other embedded parts.

The Stranger crouched down to pet the dogs.

Loac shouted, "Hey!"

The Stranger turned to look at Loac, his face unreadable.

Loac walked towards The Stranger, his steps pounding the cobblestones as he approached the man.

Without hesitation, Loac bellowed, "What are you doing with my dogs?!"

The Stranger remained unflinching.

Loac saw that a strong jawline framed his rugged face, and his hair was a tangled mess of brown waves that fell just before his shoulders.

The Stranger's eyes were stern and unflinching.

As The Stranger rose, Loac noticed the armour was torn. It had slipped slightly off his shoulders, revealing an old scar across his chest.

Loac observed blood stains on the man's armour, and he had a fresh claw mark on his chest.

The Stranger began walking towards the side of the baker's shop, and Loac couldn't help but be curious as to whether he was the mysterious Stranger from Vinenoris who saved the young girl's life; who was this Stranger and why was he in Cruatan with a fresh wound on his chest?

Loac followed The Stranger, but when he got to the side of the bakery, The Stranger was nowhere to be seen.

Loac stopped and scratched his head in confusion.

For a few seconds, Loac looked around, wondering where The Stranger went.

Loac then turned his attention to the dogs, who were jumping with excitement.

Loac patted them while untying them, and they licked his hands and wagged their tails with enjoyment.

Loac couldn't help but wonder if the dogs' enthusiasm was for him or The Stranger, who had just vanished.

Darkness had crept into the evening, and Loac could hear his name being yelled from a distance.

Loac recognised his parents' voices, but the urgency in their tone made him uneasy.

Loac quickened his pace, his feet pounding on the cobblestones as he walked through the village.

As soon as Loac's parents saw him on the streets, they ran towards him and embraced him tightly.

Loac's mother clung to him, her body shaking.

"Thank God you're okay," Brigid gasped.

Loac tried to wiggle free from his mother's tight embrace as confusion clouded his mind, "Yes, I am. Why?"

Opedius stepped forward, his face tense as he spoke, "The children that went missing in the forest... their bodies have been found, and they were killed in the forest by what appeared to be a Scanlist. I feared something could have happened to you."

Loac's hands trembled as his stomach churned violently after he processed the horrible news.

Loac spoke in a shaken voice, "Father, I am fine. I just got the bread and walked the dogs as you asked."

Opedius and Brigid sighed with relief as they all walked home with the dogs.

Loac noticed his parents exchanging worried looks as they gazed into the forest.

Loac couldn't help but feel a sense of foreboding, wondering what dangers lurked in the dark forest.

CHAPTER FOUR
The Hunt

Loac observed a brief pause in his father's movement, accompanied by his smile fading upon entering their home.

Opedius took a deep breath, then proceeded toward Loac with a forced, plastic smile.

Opedius said, "Loac, I think it's time we do the tracking I mentioned the other day. I am sorry—I should have done it yesterday."

Loac nodded in agreement.

"Excellent, let's venture outside," Opedius proposed.

Stepping into the embrace of the outdoors, Loac and Opedius embarked on their journey towards a rugged hill, with scattered trees making it possible to see the bright clear sky flooding the steep hill as the cool breeze gently caressed their faces.

Opedius walked attentively, studying each impression his boots left on the terrain.

Eventually, Opedius paused and stooped down, inspecting the marks in more detail.

Opedius motioned for Loac to join him.

Without hesitation, Loac mirrored his father's stance, examining the direction of his father's gaze.

Opedius, his tone calm yet firm, guided Loac's observations. "Notice the depth and the size of my print, then compare it to yours."

Opedius elaborated further, "You see, the size and depth of a footprint can provide valuable clues about who, or what, has passed by. If you spot disturbed vegetation or broken branches, these are signs that something has walked this path. Similarly, a flock of birds fluttering away could indicate the nearby presence of a predator. Always stay aware of any rustling of leaves or snapping of twigs, as these noises can help locate a predator or its prey."

Loac nodded, his focus unwavering, fully engrossed in his father's instructions.

Once their session concluded, Opedius prompted Loac to feed the chickens while he went inside their cottage to speak with Brigid.

Loac nodded and headed to the chicken pen on their property.

Loac detoured to the small wooden shed against the enclosure, retrieving the satchel of chicken feed before returning to the chicken pen.

Loac began distributing the feed among the eager chickens.

As twilight settled, the encroaching darkness took the sun's fading glory.

Suddenly, a harsh screech sliced through the silence from the heart of the neighbouring forest, prickling Loac's skin with goosebumps.

Cathal whimpered in anxiety while Finn launched into an aggressive volley of barks.

Loac gently placed the feed sack down, rushing towards the distressed dogs in the dog pen next to where Loac was.

"Easy, boys, easy. There's no reason to be scared," Loac consoled them, his tone a blend of reassurance and calmness.

Loac unlatched the creaky wooden gate, his hands brushing against the weathered wire.

As soon as the gate opened, Cathal barrelled into Loac with a force that sent Loac sprawling on the ground.

Unfazed, the dog bolted into the foreboding forest towards the source of the screech, with Finn hot on his heels.

Loac charged after them, scrambling to his feet, his heart pounding in sync with his footsteps.

"Cathal, Finn, please come back!" Loac pleaded into the quiet wilderness, his voice echoing ominously.

Drawn deeper into the forest by Cathal's echoing barks, Loac found the underbrush growing denser, the sunlight failing to pierce through.

As Loac closed the distance, a rank odour invaded his nostrils, a vile cocktail of blood and decay that grew more potent with every stride.

Loac tentatively traced its origin, and a chilling sight met his gaze.

A figure Loac couldn't quite distinguish lay on the forest floor—a carcass of some sort.

Gathering his courage, Loac raced towards it.

Approaching the chilling spectacle, Loac expelled a breath—a once formidable wolf, now reduced to a gruesome, lifeless heap.

A shudder rippled through Loac's body, goosebumps all over his skin as the horrifying realisation dawned on him.

Something out there was capable of this horrific act against a potent predator.

"Cathal, Finn, where are you?" Loac bellowed, his voice frantic.

Loac's eyes caught the sight of wolf's paw prints nearby.

The air carried an unfamiliar metallic tang of blood, and traces of red were scattered chaotically on the ground.

Another set of paw prints, much more significant and deeply etched into the earth, aroused Loac's concern.

The size and depth suggested a creature of immense size and weight.

Loac's body tightened with apprehension, his heart drumming a frantic rhythm in his chest.

Finn's whimpering cut through the eerie quiet, drawing his attention.

Loac found Finn and Cathal locked in a stare into the forest's deeper gloom, their tails tucked low and ears flat, deaf to Loac's calls.

Urgency overcame Loac, and he started running but was abruptly jerked back.

Loac attempted to resist, a startled cry ripping from his throat until he recognised the grip—it was his father.

Opedius shouted furiously, "I told you never to go into the forest! It is not safe. Why did you go into the forest after what I told you? You could have got yourself killed!"

Loac tried to fight back the tears, and then he broke away from his father's grasp.

Seeing his father glaring at him, Loac's body trembled as he shouted back.

"I am sorry. The dogs escaped from the pen, and I wanted to bring them home. I didn't want something to happen to them."

Opedius warned sternly, "Even if it seems safe, you must not enter the forest for any reason, even to rescue the dogs. Do you understand me?"

Loac nodded silently.

Heavy, ominous steps followed a fearsome roar that shattered the relative quiet.

The Scanlist, a monstrous creature the size of a bear, emerged from the shelter of the shadowed trees.

Loac's scream threatened to break free, but Opedius covered his mouth, muffling the cry of terror.

Opedius positioned himself protectively in front of Loac.

The Scanlist, with its pitch-black fur and snake-like tail dragging along the ground, moved on all fours. Its black and yellow eyes pierced through the darkness.

It stalked menacingly between the trees, encircling the terrified pair.

Its attention seemed concentrated on the floor as it searched for something until its gaze landed on Loac.

With a terrifying growl, it lunged towards Loac, but Opedius intercepted the creature, brandishing the wolf's broken bone as a weapon.

The Scanlist swatted Opedius away with a mighty sweep of its tail, knocking Opedius to the ground.

The creature advanced slowly towards Opedius, its teeth bared in a threatening hiss.

A terrified scream finally escaped Loac's lips, Loac's body trembling, frozen in fear as he witnessed his father helpless on the ground.

Just as the Scanlist was about to pounce, a distant roar and the metallic tang of unfamiliar blood filled the air.

Distracted, the Scanlist glanced towards the source of the sound, shot a last glance at Opedius, then bounded into the forest, towards the roar and the scent of fresh blood.

Groaning, Opedius rose from the forest floor, rushing to Loac, Opedius's face etched with panic.

Loac remained rooted to the spot, speechless, his eyes wide with shock.

Opedius quickly scooped up Loac, then whistled sharply for the dogs.

Cathal and Finn immediately obeyed, turning away from the forest and running past Opedius and Loac.

Their pace quickened as they made their way towards the safety of home.

Racing into their home, Opedius was panting heavily, his grip on Loac unyielding.

Opedius was so immersed in his panic that he didn't immediately register the familiar surroundings of their cottage.

The commotion drew Brigid from the kitchen.

Brigid saw an exhausted Opedius, and a shaken Loac, her eyes widening in alarm.

Gently, Opedius set Loac down, instructing him in a strained voice to go to his bedroom.

Without uttering a word, Loac obediently complied.

Opedius turned to Brigid, his eyes conveying the gravity of the situation.

"A Scanlist nearly took Loac from us today. If it hadn't been distracted, I might not have been able to save him. We can't stay in this village anymore; it's not safe for us. I'll speak to Osloaf. Perhaps he and his comrades can escort us out of here."

Brigid nodded in acquiescence, her expression grave.

Opedius continued, "We must pack tonight, salvaging whatever valuables we have. Osloaf's assistance will come at a significant cost, unfortunately. We need to be prepared. Brigid, go to the bakery and get whatever else we need. There is no time to waste."

Chapter Five
Osloaf

Opedius found himself standing before Osloaf's rustic cottage, a simple structure of timber and clay.

The lush and untamed front lawn swayed in the cool breeze that caressed Opedius' face.

The serene stillness of the night was only disturbed by the chirping of crickets, their melodies weaving a lullaby for the twilight.

Opedius raised a hand, knocking on the sturdy wooden door with a firm thud.

The door creaked open, revealing Osloaf.

Osloaf had a lean yet sturdy physique, with neatly cropped brown hair that framed the old scar on his right eyebrow.

Osloaf attire was a stark black surcoat gracefully cascading over his plackart, gauntlet-clad hands at his sides, and thick-soled black boots.

The serene quietness was interrupted by his voice, which had a gravelly undertone and lacked warmth.

"What do you want?" Osloaf demanded.

Opedius responded, "I direly need your services. My family and I require an escort to Caniton. Cruatan is no longer a safe haven. The Scanlist has reappeared, and the forest is becoming increasingly dangerous. I fear for my son's safety if we remain here. Caniton will be safer. Could you assist us?"

At this, Osloaf laughed derisively.

"Caniton? That insipid place? A settlement filled with spineless individuals who rarely leave the safety of their dwellings. How on earth do you think you will be safe there?"

Opedius held his gaze steady as he responded. "That is precisely my point. If that village were ever attacked, it would be a slaughter. But no attacks from monsters or bandits have happened like that in that village. The people are so scared to do anything, especially to my family, and the walls and guards will keep my son from venturing too far."

A pause hung in the air.

Osloaf nodded slowly and said, "It's only a matter of time before your son ventures beyond Caniton and encounters dangers as grave as the Scanlist. Do you presume you can keep a constant watch?"

Opedius lowered his gaze and responded, "I am aware of that, but at least in Caniton, I would have the time to equip him with all the knowledge and skills I possess. His chances of survival would certainly be better there than here."

Opedius implored, "Will you aid us?"

Osloaf gave a curt nod.

"Very well. I'll discuss it with my comrades and come up with a plan. However, our services come at a price, half of which must be paid upfront."

Opedius paused momentarily, taking a deep breath, before asking, "How much?"

"Fifty coins as an advance and the other fifty once we reach Caniton," Osloaf stated.

Opedius exhaled slowly. "Thank you. I'll return later. I have matters to attend to at home."

With that, Opedius left Osloaf and began the journey home.

When Opedius arrived at the house, Brigid ran to hear the news. "What did Osloaf say?"

Opedius replied, "He needs to discuss my proposition with his comrades now. I will revisit him in the morning, but it will cost us one hundred coins, and he wants half the payment before we leave."

"Agh!" Brigid gasped, lifting her hand against her mouth in disbelief.

"We don't have that kind of money."

Opedius responded, "We have no choice. Please gather our valuable things; we will have to sell everything. We must travel light, so we should sell everything we cannot bring."

Brigid nodded.

Brigid gathered all their jewellery and slowly took off her wedding ring.

Opedius saw the hesitation in Brigid's eyes, but with a swift move, he took off his wedding ring.

"We can always get another one. The main thing is we'll be safe; most importantly, Loac will be safe," Opedius tried to reassure her.

Brigid nodded, with tears appearing in her eyes as she gathered food, plates, ornaments, and medicines and put them in the hay wagon.

At the same time, Opedius went to visit the herbalist, the armoury, the small local shop, and the baker to get supplies and sell off all of their belongings.

Opedius woke up in the middle of the night with his eyes forced open.

Opedius's body was drenched in sweat, and his chest tightened.

Opedius's heartbeat was fast, as if it was about to burst out of his chest.

Opedius could sense something wasn't right.

Opedius rushed out of bed, changed, and ran to Osloaf's cottage.

As Opedius neared the hut, he could hear Osloaf's men arguing amongst themselves.

Opedius ran over to Osloaf's cottage and bashed through its door.

Opedius could see that Osloaf wasn't around.

All his weapons were gone, and the cupboards were emptied.

Opedius' heart sank, and his chest tightened even more.

Opedius then rushed over to Osloaf's men, sitting at the table near Osloaf's cottage, and yelled, trying to withhold his anger, "Do you know where Osloaf is?"

A burly man, one of Osloaf's comrades, rose to his feet.

His wild beard framed his face, and his heavy armour strained to contain his belly. As he swayed, his armour clinked.

The man grumbled.

"We don't know where that coward is. He ran off. You know what," the man cackled, "he never even planned on helping you and your family at all. His plan was that he would lie to you, and we all would leave the village, and your coins would be split between us," said the man with a sneer. "But that little weasel just left without telling us!"

The man lowered himself to the table and shouted, "Now, get lost!!"

Opedius' fists clenched.

Opedius was poised to strike this man but knew he had to control himself.

With a final scowl, Opedius turned and fled, his mind racing.

Opedius burst through the door of his humble home.

Opedius spotted Brigid slumped on a stool and staring off into space.

Without a word, Opedius blurted out, "That lying weasel Osloaf left the village; he tricked us!"

The words hung in the air as Opedius tried to process the situation.

Brigid shook her head, and confused, she asked in a quivering voice, "What are we going to do now? We need to leave this village now."

Opedius' voice wavered as he tried to compose himself.

"Yes, I agree. We should still leave tomorrow as planned. We must take the risk, but we must gather more weapons now that we are on our own. Let's rest so we can think clearly in the morning."

CHAPTER SIX

From Within the Shadows

Opedius clutched Loac's hand tightly as they darted through the dense forest, with Brigid following closely behind.

The sound of thundering footsteps shattered the eerie silence, and Opedius knew some monstrous creature was pursuing them.

As they pushed deeper into the woods, a thick haze of smoke filled the air, stinging their eyes and making breathing hard.

Suddenly, a flickering orange light caught Opedius' eye, and as he turned to look, he felt his stomach drop in horror.

Flames licked at the surrounding trees, closing in from all sides.

Just then, a bloodcurdling screech echoed through the forest.

Opedius gasped for air as he forced his eyes open.

Opedius mind was a whirlwind of fear and confusion.

At that moment, Opedius realised he had been dreaming; they were still at home.

Opedius turned his head and saw that Brigid was already awake, her eyes wide with alarm.

The panicked shouting from the villagers outside filled the room, and Opedius and Brigid exchanged a brief, worried glance before leaping out of bed and charging through the door of Loac's room.

They saw Loac curled up in the room's corner, hiding between the end of his bed and his wardrobe.

Loac was crying, his body shaking while his hands clenched the top of his knees, rocking back and forth.

Brigid ran to Loac and thumped down next to him. Brigid held Loac tight while kissing his head.

Tears streamed down Brigid's face as she gazed at Opedius. "I'll stay here with Loac," Brigid cried, her voice choked with emotion.

Opedius ran over to Brigid and Loac and held them tight while kissing them both on their heads. "Everything will be okay. I need to see what is happening. Please stay here. I love you both so much. You both mean everything to me."

Opedius kissed them both while trying to hold back his tears. "I need to see what is happening and try to stop whatever it is so we can all leave here safely. I love you both so much."

Before darting out of the room, Opedius cast one last lingering gaze at Brigid and Loac, their faces etched with concern.

Brigid clutched Loac tightly, her lips silently forming the words, 'I love you too'.

Opedius sprinted through the muddy terrain, his eyes darting frantically as he scanned the wooden shed enclosure.

The sharp cries of the neighbours echoed through the darkness as he desperately sought a weapon to arm himself.

A glimmer of hope flooded Opedius's mind as his gaze settled on an axe, and he tightly seized it in his sweating palms.

Opedius was determined to reach the source of the desperate screams.

As Opedius pushed forward, his foot became entangled, and he stumbled to the ground, overwhelmed by a surge of anguish.

Then, a grim realisation gripped Opedius as he gazed down upon the horrifying sight beneath him.

The mangled remains of his beloved dogs, Cathal and Finn, were the cause of his stumble.

The scene pierced Opedius' heart, inflicting profound sorrow upon him.

Opedius's body was tense, his hands gripping the axe tightly, and his grief propelled him forward.

A piercing hiss slashed through the cold air.

Opedius instantly pivoted towards the direction of the hiss.

His eyes widened, the frantic pounding of his heart threatening to break free from his ribcage.

There it was—the fearsome Scanlist, casting a monstrous shadow at Opedius's cottage door.

Its serpentine tongue flicked out.

Opedius instinctively roared, "Hey, hey!" and furiously clashed his axe against the muddy ground.

The beast's gaze was furious, its yellow and black eyes radiating the cold intent as it lunged towards him.

With a surge of adrenaline, Opedius avoided the assault.

The Scanlist bared its fangs in a snarl, sending droplets of saliva spinning into the icy air.

Opedius gripped his weapon tightly, his gaze immersed in the beast.

Opedius axe sliced through the Scanlist's thick coat in a swift move.

The beast retaliated, striking Opedius and sending him sprawling on the ground, the axe slipping from Opedius's grasp.

Opedius sprung back to his feet and reclaimed his weapon, his attention locked back onto the Scanlist, bracing for its next move.

A chilling hiss emanated from the beast, only to be drowned by the terrified screams of Brigid.

Opedius' heart skipped a beat as he turned to see the horrified expression on Brigid's face.

Tears streamed down Opedius's cheeks, the weight of the realisation pressing down on him: this might be the last time he'd ever see her.

In anguish, Opedius cried out, "Get back inside!"

Opedius spun around to face the monster.

But in a momentary lapse, a stinging pain radiated from Opedius's stomach, his eyes drawn down to see his tunic stained a dark red, oozing blood.

An unbearable pain brought him to his knees and stole his breath.

Through blurred vision and the sting of tears, Opedius lifted his gaze to Brigid, his voice barely more than a whisper, "I love you both..."

As the encroaching darkness claimed him, Opedius crumpled to the ground.

Brigid slammed the front door shut, muffled her sobs, and tried to ignore the searing pain flashing through her chest.

Brigid rushed into Loac's bedroom, scooping him up from the floor, holding him close, and kissing him fiercely.

The Scanlist's growl erupted through their cottage as the sounds of its claws scratched against the timber floor.

Chills ran down Brigid's spine.

Brigid quickly opened the wardrobe door and tucked Loac inside, her eyes welling with tears.

Brigid brushed Loac's hair from his face with a trembling hand and whispered, "Listen to me, my love. You must stay here and keep yourself safe. Whatever happens outside, don't make a sound. Please don't leave this wardrobe until you know it's safe.

Your father and I love you more than anything, and we want you to be safe. Promise me you'll take care of yourself."

Brigid's voice broke with emotion as she spoke, and tears streamed down her face, but she forced herself to be strong for her son.

Brigid kissed Loac one final time and got up.

Brigid felt Loac grab her by the arm and hug her tightly. "Mother, where are you going? Don't go."

Brigid steeled herself from her son's grasp. "I'll have to. I need to make sure the Scanlist doesn't find you. Stay here. We love you, and we'll protect you."

Brigid closed the wardrobe door and bolted out of the room, her eyes scanning frantically for the Scanlist.

Yet, it was nowhere to be found. Its sinister presence had vanished, leaving only the terrifying view of deep gouges marring the living area.

Brigid risked a cautious glance outside.

The coast seemed clear.

Brigid heart pounded in her chest as she darted towards the fallen Opedius.

Seeing Opedius motionless, she choked back a sob, her heart heavy with mounting grief.

With trembling hands, Brigid retrieved the discarded axe.

Without warning, the Scanlist emerged from the shadows.

It lunged at Brigid, its powerful swipe sending her sprawling onto the ground.

Brigid lay there, bleeding from her head and the deep gash on her back where the creature's claws had pierced her flesh.

Brigid let out one final, bloodcurdling scream before slipping into unconsciousness.

Chapter Seven
The Destruction of Cruatan

The wardrobe door creaked as Loac cautiously emerged from it, Loac's heart racing as he exhaled an icy breath. Loac paused as the chirps of crickets flooded the room.

Treading softly, Loac ventured to the living area of the house, his eyes searching frantically through the living room and widened at the sight of toppled furniture and claw marks embedded into the floor.

With another deep breath, Loac walked cautiously as he exited the cottage.

As Loac stepped out, his body froze when his eyes caught sight of the Scanlist engaged in a vicious battle with a man.

The Scanlist patrolled around the man with a vicious snarl and lunged at the man, who swiftly swung his sword, repelling the attack.

Involuntarily, a scream escaped Loac's throat.

The Scanlist turned its attention to Loac, narrowed its eyes and hurtled toward him.

Loac sealed his eyes shut, his trembling body remaining frozen.

The piercing cries of the Scanlist sliced through Loac's ears.

Loac quickly opened his eyes, only to witness a blood-stained sword slicing through the Scanlist's chest.

The lifeless creature fell to the ground as the sword was removed, revealing The Stranger whom Loac had seen before.

Exhausted, The Stranger collapsed to the ground.

Seizing the opportunity, Loac retreated inside his living area, seeking refuge.

Loac hid under a wobbly wooden table, his body shivering with fear.

Eventually, footsteps echoed on the hardwood floors, and The Stranger shouted, "Boy? Where are you, Boy? It's okay. I promise I won't hurt you."

Loac clenched his jaw to stifle his sobs and sat still under the table, not daring to move.

The Stranger shouted, "Come out, Boy. Please, don't be afraid. It's not safe to stay here. I'll protect you, but please come out from wherever you are hiding."

Loac remained frozen in hiding as The Stranger's mud-soaked feet moved around the cottage.

The footsteps halted right before Loac and The Stranger's face appeared.

The Stranger reached down and grabbed Loac's arm, but Loac fought back, sinking his teeth into The Stranger's flesh.

The Stranger recoiled, cursing under his breath.

The Stranger took a deep breath and lowered himself to Loac's level, gazing into Loac's eyes.

The Stranger's voice softened as he reached to take Loac's hand.

"Please come with me, boy," The Stranger said. "It's too dangerous here. I will protect you."

Loac hesitated momentarily, then nodded, placing his hand in The Stranger's hand and rising to his feet.

Loac blurted out, his voice cracking with fear. "I can't leave... what about my parents and dogs? Did you see them?"

The Stranger's face fell, and he lowered his head. "I'm sorry," he mumbled. "I didn't see any human or animals alive besides that Scanlist. I'm afraid they're gone."

At these words, a wave of grief washed over Loac, who stood still, frozen, staring at The Stranger in the eyes, trying to process what he had just said.

"Come on, Boy. We must go now," The Stranger said as he moved.

The Stranger winced in pain, putting his hand on the side of his hip and lifting his hand, which was covered in blood.

The Stranger turned to Loac. "I need to get medical treatment and other supplies for our journey. I need to go to the herbal store."

Loac nodded.

The Stranger let out a heavy breath, his face lined with pain.

Loac felt The Stranger grab him by the side the moment they left the cottage, guiding him behind The Stranger.

The Stranger started whistling loudly.

Loac shouted, "What are you doing?"

The Stranger ignored Loac.

They could hear the loud noise of something rushing towards them, getting louder and closer.

Loac's body shook as he peered out cautiously from behind The Stranger.

The powerful, reverberating vibrations of a horse's hooves thudded against the ground as the horse emerged from the forest, answering The Stranger's call.

The horse suddenly stopped in front of The Stranger as Loac felt The Stranger lifting him onto the back of the horse and saw The Stranger carefully taking off his black hooded cloak and placing it over Loac's head, restricting Loac's view.

The Stranger grasped the horse's bridle, leading them through the deserted Cruatan village.

"Don't look around," The Stranger cautioned, his voice low and urgent. "Just focus on the horse's mane."

Loac, however, ignored the warning, pushed the hood out of his eyes and desperately began scanning the village for his parents.

The lingering smell of charred embers permeated the village, accompanied by the squawks of crows overhead.

Loac saw with horror the lifeless bodies of his neighbours, his throat tightening with anguish.

Swiftly redirecting his gaze to the horse's mane, Loac heeded The Stranger's previous request.

Overwhelmed with emotion, he stared through the strands of the horse's mane, refusing to dwell on the fate that befell his village and family.

Suddenly, the horse came to a halt.

Lifting his gaze, Loac realised they had stopped in front of Osloaf's cottage.

Loac turned his attention to The Stranger, who met his gaze and spoke sternly, "I need to check this hut for supplies. Stay on the horse and alert me if you notice anything. I will come out if anything happens."

At that moment, an ear-piercing roar from a Scanlist ripped through the icy air, causing Loac's eyes to widen in terror as he tightened his grip on the horse.

With swift precision, The Stranger spun around, striking the horse's rear abruptly and setting it into a frightened gallop with Loac still mounted.

Desperately clinging onto the horse, Loac managed to steal one last look at The Stranger before the horse galloped on, and The Stranger's figure got smaller and smaller until he disappeared entirely from view.

Then Loac focused straight into the dark, eerie forest before him.

Without warning, the horse skidded to an abrupt stop, the surprise nearly jolting Loac from his seat.

As Loac lifted his gaze, he was met with an enveloping darkness.

Gradually, his eyes adapted to the darkness while a chilling, howling wind brushed his face, and goosebumps prickled on his skin.

Slowly, Loac dismounted; the hooting owls and rustling leaves engulfed him as he took a deep, calming breath.

Loac stepped further into the forest.

The wind's roar amplified, morphing the gentle hoots of owls into the harsh cawing of crows.

Unseen presences seemed to follow him, intensifying his sense of unease.

The forest felt alive and watchful, and a sudden shiver ran down Loac's spine as his hands grew clammy.

A sudden commotion among the leaves startled a flock of birds into flight, their shrill cries slicing through the air.

Before Loac could react, an icy hand clasped over his mouth, silencing his startled gasp; a soft, deep voice murmured in his ear, "Be calm; I will not harm you."

The hand released him, and Loac spun around, his nerves melting away as he recognised The Stranger.

The Stranger lifted Loac effortlessly onto the horse.

After securely positioning Loac in the saddle, The Stranger climbed onto the horse's back and urged it into a steady trot.

As they moved, The Stranger spoke, "I will take you to the town of Veritan."

"It's one of the few places I know where you'll be taken care of."

Confused, Loac queried, "Why can't I stay with you?"

The Stranger expelled a heavy sigh. "I'm a nomad," he confessed. "I don't have a home or a safe place for a young boy like you. You'll be much safer in Veritan. The people there are kind and will take care of you. They also owe me a favour."

The Stranger seized the reins, nudged the horse's flank with his leg, and commanded, "Hyah!"

The horse surged forward, carrying them deeper into the mysteries of the forest.

CHAPTER EIGHT
Newfound Journey

The sun set as they travelled through the dense forest, casting a warm orange and pink glow across the sky.

The trees towering above them seemed to stretch endlessly into the sky, their leaves rustling in the gentle breeze.

A chorus of chirping crickets and singing birds echoed throughout the woods.

As the horse trudged through the forest, Loac couldn't help but notice the occasional rustling in the bushes.

Suddenly, a pure white wolf emerged from the thicket, its fur glinting like moonlight and its ears sharply pointed.

The wolf's gaze locked onto The Stranger, and the two remained in a tense standoff for a few moments.

Loac uttered a startled cry against his will, drawing the wolf's attention to him.

The wolf lowered its ears and licked its lips but soon returned its gaze to The Stranger before disappearing back into the brush.

Loac's eyes widened in amazement. "I've never seen a wolf like that before!"

The Stranger turned to Loac with a small smile. "White wolves are rare and beautiful creatures. They are the protectors of these forests. Luckily, we did not pose a threat to it, and it left us alone. Let's hope it stays that way."

The Stranger looked back at where the white wolf had emerged before leading deeper into the forest.

They came upon the cliff, towering high above the forest. Its rocky face jutted out from the trees, its edges seemingly endless, creating a natural barrier between the forest and the sky.

The Stranger guided the horse towards a small clearing at the top of the cliff, where they would rest for the night.

Once they reached the top of the cliff, The Stranger jumped off the horse, grabbed Loac and lowered him to the ground.

The Stranger declared, "We will camp here for the night. I shall gather up the wood so that I can make a fire. Can you please stay here next to Sage?"

Loac scratched his head. "Sage?"

The Stranger scoffed. "Sage is the horse's name."

The Stranger retrieved an axe from Sage's saddlebag and carefully removed it to lighten the horse's load.

The Stranger walked towards a nearby tree and grunted as he struck the axe hard against the trunk.

The Stranger continued to chop away at the branches, and trunk until it fell to the ground.

After cutting the trunk into pieces, The Stranger gathered them and returned to Loac.

As The Stranger arranged the wood pieces for a fire, he noticed Loac had fallen asleep on Sage's stomach.

The Stranger smiled and chuckled softly before retrieving a small blanket from the saddlebag and covering Loac.

With his sword at his side, The Stranger leaned against a tree and watched over Loac as he slept soundly.

The Stranger glanced at Loac with a smile before sighing, and gradually, his eyes closed.

A loud noise jolted The Stranger awake.

The Stranger hand instinctively reached for his sword as he looked around for Loac, only to find he was missing.

Panic set in as The Stranger shouted, "Boy, where are you?"

Loac's voice responded from a short distance away, "I am here."

Relieved but frustrated, The Stranger stormed towards Loac and raised his voice as he glared at Loac, "You can't be wandering off by yourself. Do you have any idea how dangerous it is here? You need to stay close to me, listen to whatever I say, and obey; otherwise, you could get hurt or killed. Do you understand?"

Loac's voice trembled as he replied, "Sorry, Sir. Sage looked hungry and thirsty, so I wanted to find him some berries, that is all. I didn't venture too far."

The Stranger rolled his eyes and grunted, "Come boy, we must keep moving."

After gathering their belongings, they extinguished the fire with water before leaving the camp.

The Stranger helped Loac onto the horse and mounted behind him as they continued their journey towards Veritan.

After a few minutes of uncomfortable silence.

Loac's curiosity got the better of him, and he broke the silence. "What is your name, Sir?"

The Stranger replied, "It's Slaith."

"I never heard that name before. My name is Loac. Where are you from?" Loac asked.

Slaith softly replied in a deep voice, "I come from the kingdom called Xanitant."

Loac started speaking, his voice choked with emotion, "I've heard of that place. My father always promised he'd take me there one day. He told tales of a vibrant, beautiful kingdom that people who came from all over the world to visit that kingdom."

A soft laugh escaped Slaith's lips as he spoke. "Yes, the kingdom is beautiful and sprawling. The townhouses reach as high as the tallest trees, while swarms of people always walk throughout the streets. Every Sunday, performers would put on a grand show. I remember watching those shows with my parents as a child. I always loved them and got excited to see performers who put on shows where king knights would win back their kingdom against a massive army from the south."

Slaith's reminiscing faded into a sigh. His tone grew sombre, "As I got older, I recognised the true cost behind the kingdom's wealth."

Intrigued, Loac inquired, "What do you mean?"

Slaith explained, "A few days before I found you, Loac, I visited Vinenoris, your neighbour's village, where I saved a young girl."

Loac interjected excitedly, "I heard about that and thought that was you!"

Nodding, Slaith continued, "Yes, it was me. When I returned the girl to her mother, she pleaded with me to help ward off or slay any beasts that lurked nearby. You see, they used to have guards from Xanitant, but their king was consumed by greed and refused to despatch his men without full payment. He showed little regard for the village's potential destruction and the villagers' safety."

Loac exhaled softly, digesting Slaith's words.

A respectful silence filled the air as they continued their journey.

Sunlight pierced through the covering of leaves above, casting a spotted pattern on the path ahead.

The rustle of the underbrush, the chirping of birds, and the clopping of the horse's hooves filled the air.

Loac spoke, "Why did you call your horse, Sage?"

Loac continued, "Is it because he's a wise horse?"

Slaith remained silent, but Loac asked again, "Why did you name the horse Sage?"

Slaith grunted, lowering his head. "The name Sage reminds me of my wife, whom I cared for, who is no more. She loved the sage flower because of the smell, and green was her favourite colour."

Slaith lifted his head and chuckled as he remembered her, and he continued, "She loved them so much that she had covered our house with sage flowers, making the house smell like flowers. It infuriated me! All I wanted to do was destroy the flowers, but I couldn't bring myself to destroy them, as I knew she loved them so much. I didn't want to upset her, so I named the horse Sage, which reminds me of her."

Loac said sadly, "You must have cared for her because that was the first time I saw you laugh. She must have been a lovely lady."

"Yes, she was," Slaith replied softly.

Loac asked, "Can you tell me more about her?"

Slaith shook his head. "That is a tale for another day."

"Okay, Sir," Loac said, respecting his privacy wishes.

Slaith said, "We must find a safe place to rest and get food. Loac, can you look around and see if any hills are high?"

Loac nodded. Loac scanned the area, his vision obscured by the dense fog.

After a moment, Loac pointed to a high hill on the left. "I see a hill over there," he said with certainty.

Slaith followed Loac's direction and saw the mountain in the distance.

Slaith urged Sage toward it, confident it would provide a safe resting place.

As they reached the top of the hill, Slaith dismounted Sage, ready to help Loac down, but Loac insisted and dismounted himself.

Slaith stepped back, but not too far to catch Loac if he fell.

Once Loac dismounted the horse, Slaith spoke, "We need to gather firewood."

Loac questioned, "Fine, Sir. Which trees are the best for firewood?"

Slaith responded, "Any wood, as long as it is safe to cut from the tree, they do the same thing. You should stay near Sage because I don't want to worry about you getting hit by the tree when I cut it down."

As Loac moved toward Sage, the horse became agitated, its neighs slicing through the quiet air.

Slaith immediately unsheathed his sword.

With his free hand, Slaith shielded Loac, pushing Loac behind him as he cautiously retreated towards a nearby tree, ears straining for any hint of danger amidst the rustling leaves.

Through the wind, Slaith could hear a strange noise, as if someone or something were circling them.

Suddenly, a bloodcurdling screech pierced through the air, its discordant notes causing Loac to tremble.

Never losing his grip on Loac, Slaith led him in a controlled backward march until Loac's back was against a tree.

Swiftly, Slaith set his sword on the mossy ground, hoisting Loac onto a low-hanging branch.

Reclaiming his sword, Slaith glanced at Loac momentarily and shouted, "Climb, boy!"

Slaith stared back into the forest, listening to the noise, hoping to find the creature's location.

Another screech tore through the air, and Slaith's grip on his sword tightened.

In a flurry of movement, a Wolagist emerged from the trees and lunged at Slaith, who braced himself and nimbly side-stepped the assault.

Slaith retaliated with a fierce slash, the blade slicing its skin and drawing an enraged roar from the beast.

Yet, the Wolagist retaliated with a vicious swipe with its paw, sending Slaith spiralling backwards.

Slaith's back slammed against a tree, the impact rattling his bones just as the Wolagist prepared for another assault.

Suddenly, Slaith plucked a potion from his pocket, hurling it at the beast's face.

The Wolagist howled in anguish as the harsh liquids singed its eyes, creating an opportunity for Slaith.

Slaith plunged his sword into the Wolagist's chest, silencing it once and for all.

Loac's gaze fell upon Slaith as Loac carefully descended from the tree, concern on his face.

Loac's voice trembled as he asked, "Are you okay?"

Through gritted teeth, Slaith groaned in agony. "I'll survive."

They trudged back to camp together, where Slaith summoned enough strength to ignite a fire before stumbling towards Sage's saddle.

Slaith retrieved a selection of herbs and a bowl, lowering himself beside Sage to begin crushing the medicine.

Entranced, Loac perched beside Slaith, mesmerised by his skilled hands.

Once the herbal concoction was complete, Slaith rose with painstaking effort, limping towards the fire with the sword loosely held in his grasp. With a grunt, he placed the sword atop the fire, leaving it to heat amidst the licking flames.

Upon returning to Loac, Slaith collapsed.

With a laboured breath, Slaith turned his gaze to Loac. "Can you press the heated blade to my wounds? Afterwards, apply the mixture I made to prevent infection," Slaith instructed.

Loac nodded solemnly, his tiny hands trembling as they applied the searing blade to Slaith's injuries.

Slaith's tortured scream tore the air before he fell unconscious.

Fear overtook Loac as he called Slaith's name, his voice shaking.

Tears welled in his eyes.

Discarding the sword, Loac scrambled towards Slaith, shaking him gently in a desperate bid for a response.

Loac bent down, placing his ear against Slaith's chest, hearing the reassuring thump of a heartbeat.

The sensation of the steady pulse flooded Loac with relief.

Loac stood, rushing to retrieve a blanket from Sage's saddle bag.

Once Loac found it, he draped it tenderly over Slaith.

Armed with Slaith's sword—a weighty burden in his tiny hands—Loac took a vigilant position with his back against a tree, unaware that he was replicating what Slaith had done the previous night.

Loac faced Slaith but also maintained a clear view of the forest.

Loac inspected the handle of the sword again, looking at the detail of the different types of objects carved in the hold, smiling slightly when he saw the Gnomon.

Loac had memories of his father waking him up early.

One day, Loac got so annoyed about waking up so early that he grabbed the sundial and hid it in his room to get a few more hours of sleep, but he forgot to put it back.

When his father discovered what Loac had done, he woke him up earlier as punishment.

Loac never hid his father's sundial again.

Loac's eyes mirrored Slaith's steely gaze from the previous night as he stared into the enigmatic depths of the forest.

The sun came up, and Slaith suddenly woke up.

Slaith panicked and put his hand to his side, hoping to find the sword.

Slaith then looked down and saw the blanket.

Peeling it off him, Slaith started to look around.

"You're finally awake. I was beginning to think you'd never wake up," Loac remarked, his tone shifting to one of concern as his gaze landed on Slaith's wounds. "How are you feeling?"

Slaith looked at the wounds.

Slaith noticed they had stopped bleeding and looked like they had been cleaned.

Slaith didn't touch them but said, "It's a lot better. Thank you. I am sorry I passed out. You weren't safe. Anything could have…"

"There's no need for thanks. You needed the rest, and besides, everything was fine. I should get used to being on my own if I travel with you," Loac said with a smile.

Slaith let out a lengthy sigh. "Sorry, boy. You won't be travelling with me after we get to Veritan. It is unsafe here, and you will be cared for there."

Loac looked at the ground while throwing stones aimlessly. "I know, but you will still visit me, won't you, Slaith?"

Slaith sighed. "I will visit if I am passing by."

CHAPTER NINE
The Fractured Veritan

S laith pulled on the reins, bringing the horse skidding to a halt.

Dust kicked up as the horse made a soft neigh; the sounds of its hooves clattering abruptly ceased.

Slaith and Loac peered down at the Kingdom of Veritan hidden behind a towering stone wall.

The view was concealed mainly, but a smattering of town-house rooftops peeked out over the stone wall and drawbridge at the centre of the stone wall.

Slaith paused momentarily and let out a near-inaudible sigh, his gaze shifting to meet Loac's. "You will be properly cared for here, I promise you."

Slaith studied Loac's posture, who let out a deep sigh, a slight but perceptible sag in Loac's shoulders.

Yet, Loac remained silent.

With a gentle tug on the reins, Slaith urged Sage forward.

A fresh breeze caressed Slaith's face while the clear blue sky lit their path into Veritan.

Upon reaching the town, Slaith dismounted from the horse, taking hold of Sage's bridle while gently guiding Loac through the kingdom of Veritan.

"Wow," Loac whispered.

Slaith turned to look at Loac, noticing his wide-eyed expression as he scanned the tall, white-painted buildings with black wooden slates.

The edges of the buildings and the areas surrounding the windows caught Loac's attention, his expression transitioning into one of sadness.

Curious, Slaith followed Loac's gaze and observed the blackened, scorched buildings with broken windows and claw marks etched into the doors.

Loac's curiosity was evident. "What happened here?"

Slaith sighed heavily as he told the tale. "Years ago, this kingdom was once a vibrant, bustling place. It was so lively that people would travel for days to visit. They came to watch the greatest horsemen in jousting competitions to receive the finest training from experienced mentors. And to search for knowledge or to seek refuge. Many found a permanent home here, owing to a stable government that made decisions for the betterment of the people. Even when those decisions were harsh yet necessary for justice's sake, the political situation changed after some time. The old King and Queen were dethroned by the Valentat family, who were loyal followers of the kingdom of Xanitant."

Slaith's voice hinted at regret as he continued, "These new rulers were selfish and showed no care for the people. One fateful day, the town was attacked by ferocious monsters, and the new, cowardly King and Queen abandoned their people, leaving the villagers to fend for themselves."

Slaith paused in his stride, tightening his grip on the horse's bridle as he surveyed the scorched buildings around them.

"The aftermath of the attack resulted in many casualties. But a few brave and selfless individuals led the surviving villagers to safety. They provided food, tended to wounds, and shielded them from further harm while waiting for the monsters to depart. After this tragedy, the people of Veritan swore a solemn vow never to allow a King or Queen to rule their town again."

"So, what happened next, with no one to lead them?" Loac asked, curiosity piquing.

Turning to face Loac, Slaith's facial expression softened as he responded, "The people who protected them were respected and trusted by the villagers. Their guidance helped shape the vibrant town that Veritan is today. To maintain order and protect it from future attacks, many villagers trained as guards, ready to defend their home at any cost."

Loac's eyebrows rose as he queried, "And you think I'll be safe here?"

A small chuckle escaped Slaith as he caught Loac's confused expression.

"Yes, it is no longer the sanctuary it once was, but the respected leaders have ensured their town remains a safe haven.

I particularly trust one of them, a woman named Elantren. I sincerely believe she will care for you as if you were her own. She is one of the few people I trust completely."

Loac was about to speak but was interrupted by a voice calling, "Slaith".

Slaith turned to look, only to see it was Elantren. He smiled as their eyes met, and the pair slowly moved towards her.

Elantren hair was as dark as night, tied in a messy half-ponytail that cascaded down to her waist.

Elantren gown, a blend of vibrant crimson and obsidian black, had seen better days.

The once ornate fabric was now marred with grime.

Under Elantren's green, sparkling eyes, there lay grey shadows.

As they approached, Slaith hugged Elantren, and then Elantren asked, "What brings you here, Slaith?"

Slaith looked at Loac, and Elantren followed his gaze, smiling when she saw the boy. "Who is this handsome young fellow?"

Loac didn't say anything.

Slaith replied, "That boy, Loac, is the reason I am here. We should talk somewhere in private."

Elantren nodded, and they strolled away, keeping Loac in their sight.

Slaith whispered, "I saved this boy from a Scanlist that slaughtered all the people in his town Cruatan, including his parents. He has no one, and you are the only person I trust to take care of him and treat him as your own. I know it's a lot to ask, but I have no choice."

Slaith saw Elantren put her hands to her lips as she remained still, gazing into Slaith's eyes without blinking.

Elantren's gaze moved as she stared at Loac with a soft expression and nodded. "I will take good care of him until I can find a better home for him."

Slaith breathed a sigh of relief. "Thank you, Elantren."

Elantren nodded, and they both turned to walk towards Loac.

Loac dismounted Sage, and Elantren walked towards Loac and lowered herself to Loac's height, a warm smile on her face.

Elantren said, "Now, you handsome young man, you look like you need rest and food. Let me show you to your bed and get you some food."

Elantren reached out her hand to Loac, but Loac stubbornly kept his hands to his side and stared at her.

Elantren stood and said softly, "Well then, please follow me."

Slaith and Loac followed Elantren as she directed them to two rooms in her stoned castle at the very back end of the protective walls.

The castle was constructed from massive blocks of rough-hewn stone, its walls stacked high and thick, and it towered over the surrounding town.

Weathered scars marked the stony exterior.

Its size dominated every other dwelling in the city.

Once they entered the castle, Elantren guided them to their rooms and left a spare set of clothes on the bed for them both.

Loac grabbed the clothes and went to the washroom to bathe.

The bedroom, a grand two-poster bed, was swathed in damask curtains.

A red-stained candle on the hearth burned brightly, casting warm shadows on the scorched stone walls with the barely visible family crest.

The icy cold breeze swept through the cracked windows as Slaith sat on the bed.

Slaith's gaze fixed upon the bed frame, which bore the scars of fire, its edges charred and blackened.

Slaith felt the bed dip slightly as Elantren sat next to him.

Slaith lifted his gaze as he stared deeply into Elantren's bright eyes.

He smiled when her eyes met his.

Elantren whispered, "I see how you look at the young man. You seem to have grown fond of the boy, and he seems to like you. Are you sure this is the right thing to do?"

Slaith exhaled. "Being a nomad like myself is no lifestyle for a child. He has his whole life ahead of him, and I don't know if I will always be able to protect him. He already has had two close calls. At least he will stand a better chance of living here than if he were travelling with me."

Elantren nodded, and Slaith felt Elantren's hands touch him softly.

Elantren spoke gently, "I understand. I promise you I will take care of the boy. Slaith, I owe you at least that much."

Slaith nodded. "Thank you."

Slaith looked at Elantren with a sombre expression. "It's time for me to say goodbye to Loac."

Slaith walked through the stone corridor, his footsteps echoing through the corridor as he walked towards the washroom.

Slaith noticed a few people stealing glances at him and whispering amongst themselves.

It made him feel uneasy.

Slaith could hear one man saying, "I heard the man over there keep objects of everyone he killed as a kind of memento of all the innocent victims. He can't be trusted. If he doesn't go soon, we must scare him away."

The other man said, "Did you hear about the boy he brought? The boy is supposed to stay. I don't feel safe or trust the child because he came with that stranger. I am afraid of what he will do if he stays."

The first man agreed, "Yes. The child must go one way or another..."

Slaith stopped in his tracks, furious at what he heard.

Slaith marched over to the two villagers and took out his sword.

Slaith pointed the blade tip against the villager's neck and hissed through clenched teeth, "Listen, you fool. Stop making up these lies to scare people because you feel threatened and scared. Now, if I hear that something has happened to the boy or if he's harmed, you will be the first person I come after. I will cut you into pieces; your tongue will be the first part I take from you. So you can't tell any more lies. I am a man of my word, and you know what? I can show you what I am capable of, seeing as you've been exaggerating the truth for your benefit. Otherwise, you won't feel the need to be threatened by me. So, the boy must be treated like a king here. If anything less, I will come after you all."

Slaith stepped backwards, moving his sword away from the villager's neck.

The villager shouted, "You will not get away with this! The guards will kill you now for using that sword."

Slaith turned to walk away, putting his sword back in its sheath.

The villagers shouted, "Guards! Guards! The man over there with the sword threatened to kill me. He wants to kill me. Get him!"

The guards approached with their swords raised.

Their heavy armour clinked as they rushed towards Slaith, ready to attack.

While raising his hand, Slaith signalled to the guards that he wasn't armed but kept his hands close to his sword.

Slaith declared loudly, "I don't want to fight. I don't want any bloodshed."

The guards laughed. "Are you serious? We will not let you go after you threaten our people."

The guard raised his sword at Slaith. "You are coming with us to the prison cell. It's going to be your new home."

Slaith exhaled a deep breath as he reached for his sword.

Elantren screamed. "No! Stop this madness at once. No blood will be shed in this town. This man is here to drop off a young boy, a survivor from Cruatan. He is leaving now, so please, please, stop this and let him leave."

Slaith lowered his sword while keeping himself fixated on the guards.

The guards also lowered their swords. "Yes, we will do as you wish, Elantren."

They turned to Slaith. "You can go, but only because Elantren has requested it. But if you don't leave now, there will be trouble."

The guards walked away.

Slaith turned to Elantren and spoke softly as he said, "Thank you."

Elantren muttered, "I didn't do it for you. It was the guards that I was saving. And for Loac too, I say he would miss you if you couldn't visit. You will pop in to visit, won't you?"

"I hope so, but it won't be for some time." Slaith sighed and continued, "He may have forgotten me by then."

There was silence for a moment when Slaith added, "I must go before the guards change their minds."

Elantren nodded. "Take care, Slaith."

Slaith walked towards the washroom and opened the door.

Loac was getting changed when Slaith walked through the door.

With a sombre expression, Slaith looked at Loac.

Loac looked at Slaith similarly and said, "Are you saying goodbye, Slaith?"

Slaith mumbled, "Yes."

Suddenly, Loac leaped up and hugged Slaith tightly.

Loac spoke sadly. "Thank you, Slaith."

Slaith held Loac by the shoulders and pulled back slightly to look him in the eye. "No need to say any more, Loac."

Loac nodded. "Will you come and visit me?"

Slaith spoke in a hushed tone. "Yes, I will, Loac. I promise."

Slaith ruffled Loac's hair and slowly walked out of the room with his head lowered.

Loac rushed to the door and watched Slaith walk down the corridor, overhearing the villagers' comments. "That stranger is leaving now, and that little boy he brought will stay here. I want to get rid of the boy."

Fear and unease settled in Loac's heart, and he quickly donned the hooded cloak Slaith had given him earlier.

With the hood covering his face, Loac slipped out of the bedroom and stealthily through the crowds, avoiding Slaith's view.

Once outside, Loac ran towards Sage and gave the horse a comforting pat on the head. "Good boy, Sage. Now act normal."

Loac noticed there was a wooden hay wagon carriage tied to Sage.

Slaith must have put it on Sage earlier to help him gather and transport supplies for his journey.

Loac climbed into the hay wagon, hid behind the food, and covered the cloak over him, hoping to escape the village unnoticed.

A few minutes later, Loac heard Slaith's footsteps approaching, and then Slaith's voice. "Sage, it is just the two of us now."

Slaith lightly hopped onto Sage's back and set off away from Veritan and towards the forest.

After some time, Loac felt the horse coming to a halt; Loac heard Slaith dismounting Sage and his muddy footsteps trudging towards the hay wagon.

Loac tried to curl himself in a tight ball to hide behind the supplies to avoid being seen.

Bit by bit, Slaith unloaded all the supplies from the hay wagon.

Slaith saw Loac and angrily dropped what he was holding.

Slaith grabbed Loac and pulled him out of the hay wagon.

Slaith roared, "What are you doing here? I told you to stay in that town."

Loac tried to soothe him, "I know, Slaith, but I overheard the villagers talking about getting rid of me. I would have been dead if I had stayed."

Slaith grunted. "You would have been okay. Elantren would have taken care of you."

Loac replied, "Yes, maybe. If she watched me every second, I might have survived. But you know that is not possible. They fear you and were scared to harm me because of you. So, they would have probably gotten rid of me once you left, and I feel safer with you. I have no one else I can trust besides you, Slaith."

Slaith lowered his head, exhaled a deep breath when he processed the last words that Loac spoke, and then grunted. "Fine. You will stay with me for now. Off you go to feed Sage."

Relieved that Slaith was not too angry with him, Loac ran towards Sage with the hay and water.

Once Loac finished feeding Sage, Slaith said, "Let's go. It's getting late."

Loac and Slaith gathered the supplies, put them back in the hay wagon, and journeyed more profoundly into the forest.

CHAPTER TEN
The Secrets Behind the Hidden Hut

Loac and Slaith approached a wooden hut surrounded by dense foliage and towering trees, which seemed to reach the sky.

They could only hear the rustling of leaves and the occasional chirping of birds as they arrived at the small wooden hut in the middle of the forest, but not near any town.

Loac asked in a confused tone, "Is this your home, Slaith?"

"No, it isn't. I don't have a home. I visit it sometimes," Slaith answered.

Slaith dismounted from Sage.

Carrying food and water from the hay wagon, Slaith approached the hut door and knocked on it.

A man opened the door, revealing his rugged features.

The man looked over forty years old, with deep lines etched on his weathered face.

He wore a dirty jerkin and faded black pants that had seen better days.

The man's piercing brown eyes gazed out from beneath thick brows, and he had dark chestnut hair.

The most striking feature of his face was his wild beard.

The man looked at Slaith with a severe gaze and asked, "Why are you here?"

Slaith grinned at him. "You know why I am here."

The man broke out into a deep laugh, removing his serious face.

"Of course I do. Our doors are always open for you, Slaith."

He pushed the door open and invited Slaith into the house.

Inside the hut, it was much more spacious.

A cosy living area with a small table and chairs and a fireplace in the corner provided warmth and light.

To the right was a small kitchenette. To the left were two bedrooms, each with a comfortable bed and a small bedside table. At the back of the hut, there was a bathroom.

Slaith turned to Loac and shouted, "Boy, come here."

The man smiled, came forward, and quickly looked at Loac.

The man sighed with relief and then smiled again. "I thought you told me you didn't have any children."

Slaith corrected him, "Huvnor, he is not my son. I saved him when his village, Cruatan, was attacked. I saved the boy, but sadly, no one in the village survived."

Huvnor remained silent for a second with a pained expression before looking at Loac and saying, "Come, boy, we will get you out of those terrible clothes. I'll ask Alluren to prepare your room, but you can sit next to the dog. I hope you're not afraid of dogs, as I have a dog named Rex. But don't worry, he won't harm you. He may look scary, but he is a teddy bear."

Loac beamed when he heard there was a dog.

Loac quickly replied, "No, Sir. I love dogs. I had two dogs, and I called them Cathal and Finn. Can I see Rex?"

Huvnor nodded and pointed towards where Rex was lying next to the fire.

Loac quickly approached Rex, sat beside him, and patted Rex.

Rex, a tiny Cocker Spaniel, glanced at Loac before laying his head on the ground.

Huvnor then turned to Slaith and hugged him, extending his invitation. "Now, Slaith, please come inside."

Slaith grabbed Huvnor by the shoulder, directing him towards the hay wagon.

"I have gifts for you. Would you give me a hand carrying them inside?" Slaith asked, pointing to the bags at the end of the hay wagon.

Huvnor nodded and walked towards the hay wagon, helping to unpack Slaith's things.

Slaith handed Huvnor a bag full of food and a bag of coins.

"That's for you," he said.

"Thank you. I appreciate it. You don't know how much we needed this, so thank you," replied Huvnor gratefully.

Slaith and Huvnor entered the hut and sat on stools beside the table.

Huvnor asked Slaith, "Do you need a drink? Ale or something?"

Huvnor's wife, Alluren, walked out of the room.

Alluren looked like she was in her forties, with long blonde hair and bright blue eyes.

Her kind-hearted nature was evident in her warm smile and cheerful demeanour as she greeted Slaith and Loac.

"Good evening, Slaith. What's this handsome little boy's name?"

Slaith responded, "He is called Loac, Alluren."

Alluren seemed delighted. "I'm happy to see you both. Now, make yourselves comfortable while I bring out our finest ale we've been saving for your return. It's been a while since we last saw you, Slaith."

Alluren turned to Loac and smiled sweetly. "Now, little man, can I get you anything?"

Loac paused momentarily and said, "Any food would be nice."

A yawn escaped Loac's mouth.

Alluren smiled. "You seem tired. You can rest in the bedroom on the left if you like."

Loac smiled and said, "Thank you," before heading to the bedroom.

Once Loac had gone to get some rest, the three friends sat in the living area.

Alluren asked Slaith, "Do you want anything to drink?"

Slaith replied cheerfully, "Yes, please. Any ale will do. Your ale is always of the highest quality."

Alluren nodded and went to get it, and Slaith sat down.

Slaith sighed with relief, finally sitting on something comfortable beside the rocky ground or Sage's saddle.

Alluren returned with the ale and sat beside Huvnor across the table from Slaith.

Slaith asked Alluren, "I am wondering if there's anything you can do to Sage's saddle so that it doesn't feel like I am sitting on stones all the time."

Alluren laughed. "Of course. Let me look at it tomorrow. I'd say I can make something or improve it a bit."

Alluren continued, "So, how did you come across the boy? And why did you bring him here with you? Knowing you, I know it wasn't your decision. You'd barely hold a baby, so taking care of the boy is not something I can imagine."

Slaith looked at Alluren and Huvnor deeply before speaking. "Yes, you're right."

Slaith paused momentarily, taking a deep breath before continuing, "I went to Veritan, where I thought Loac would be safe to grow up and would be cared for."

Slaith leaned forward. "...but the boy refused to stay there and snuck onto the back of my hay wagon. I only found him a few hours ago."

Slaith sat back in his chair with his arms folded. "I was going to bring him back, but I saw how scared he was of the people in the village because he overheard them talking about trying to get rid of him."

Slaith's voice grew louder. "Even though I threatened those little weasels, I would kill them if anything happened to him."

Slaith's voice slowed down a bit as he spoke the following words, his gaze falling to the table, "But when I saw how scared he was, he begged me to let him stay and said he felt safe with me and had no one else. Knowing he had already gone through so much, I didn't want to be another person who left him and made him feel more scared than he was... How could I leave him knowing there was truth to what he was saying?"

Slaith looked up, meeting Alluren's eyes. "You know how cruel and desperate people can be when they feel threatened."

Huvnor grunted, "I know how people can be all too well." And he drank his ale in one full gulp this time.

Huvnor asked, "So Slaith, now that you are stuck with the boy, what are your plans with him?"

"If he stays with me, I must ensure he learns to protect himself. He won't last long otherwise." Slaith sounded firm.

Slaith continued, "First, I must go to Atanval. The place makes the lightest but most highly protective armour and weapons. I know I'd have to get armour for the boy and a smaller sword. The skinny boy can barely hold my sword; never mind, swing it! Once we get there, I will train him. And after that, I am not sure."

Alluren laughed. "You didn't fully answer the question. How did you come across the boy in the first place?"

Slaith sighed. "I visited the town of Cruatan to stock up on supplies, and I saw Loac with his parents when I was there. On my last visit, when I left, I heard screams from the village and rushed back to see what happened."

Slaith continued, "Once I got there, there was only silence. The screams had stopped, and all I saw were the remains of the villagers."

Slaith clenched his fist. "If I had stayed in the village longer, maybe I could have prevented the attack and saved Loac's parents."

Slaith continued with a heavy heart, "The poor boy was the only one left. He was so frightened that he wouldn't come out from under the kitchen table."

Slaith paused for a moment, the memory still fresh in his mind. "And he was so scared that he even bit me when I tried to help him."

Huvnor spoke softly, "Why did you live near that village?"

Slaith's jaw tensed, his voice low and filled with anger. "The Scanlist that slaughtered the town was the same one I had been hunting for years after it killed my beloved wife, Solusin. It took everything away from me."

Slaith took a deep breath, trying to calm himself before continuing, "...and it did the same thing to Loac, but it can't hurt anyone else now."

Slaith's gaze dropped to the table, his voice quiet and solemn as he explained, "I found the creature's trail while I was on a pilgrimage to lay flowers at my wife's resting place. The flowers were her favourite, and I wanted to honour her memory."

Slaith paused for a moment before looking up at Alluren and Huvnor. "That's why I was there."

Huvnor inquired, "Are you certain Loac's parents are dead? Did either you or Loac see their bodies?"

Slaith shook his head somberly. "I saw them, but fortunately, the darkness shielded Loac's sight, allowing me to lead Loac away before he could see them."

Huvnor pressed, "Did you inform Loac of what you saw?"

Slaith responded with a shake of his head.

Huvnor advised, "You should tell him, eventually."

Slaith exhaled deeply. "I will if he brings it up again. I did mention to him that I believe they're gone."

The silence that followed was heavy with grief, but it was broken by Huvnor's hand reaching over to pat Slaith's shoulder.

Huvnor's sympathetic gaze met Slaith's, offering comfort without words.

After a few seconds, Huvnor withdrew his hand and picked up his ale again.

"How long do you plan on staying here?" Huvnor asked. "You know you can stay as long as you need, my friend."

"Thank you," Slaith replied, his voice still heavy with emotion. "We won't be staying long. Just a few days to rest and heal my wound. Then we will go to Atanval."

Alluren got up and said, "I will get some water from the well; I will be back in a minute," and she walked out.

Huvnor's gaze hardened as he spoke, "I heard terrible rumours about you, Slaith before we crossed paths. You did some terrible things. Things I hope the boy will never know or see."

Slaith's expression remained neutral as he responded, "You know me better now. Have I done anything to harm you and your family?"

Slaith leaned back in his chair, folding his arms across his chest. "Many people tell lies to make themselves feel better, or maybe it's their way of manipulating people. I've encountered many terrible people who have done unspeakable things, more horrible than most monsters I have ever encountered."

Slaith paused, taking a bite of the warm bread on the table before continuing, "At least with a monster; I know they will try to kill me if we cross paths. So, I know to avoid those paths and be prepared to defend when they attack. However, it is much more dangerous with people, as I don't know their intentions. Are they friends or foes?"

Slaith's gaze locked with Huvnor's, his tone firm. "But I assure you, I will do nothing to harm you or your family. You have my word."

Slaith munched on the food before he continued, "There were many times when I would hear a scream from a child calling for help, and when I arrived to help the child in need, I would get ambushed. I would defend myself, and the woman would go back to the village and shout that I killed her people, which unfortunately is true, but she would leave out the part that I was ambushed. In reality, they probably came across and killed more people than I have."

Slaith explained, "There are only a few people you can trust. You know this to be true. Therefore, you live in the middle of the forest, away from people, rather than in a village."

Slaith turned to Huvnor and looked around the room frantically, "Where is your child?"

Huvnor chuckled. "She's quite quiet, isn't she? Alluren put her to bed just before you arrived. Sometimes, I forget she's even in the same room with us because she rarely makes a sound."

Slaith chuckled and joked. "I remember when you used to be so groomed. You always brushed your hair and even plaited your beard."

Huvnor smiled and said, "Ha, that was because my daughter Lily wanted to be a Gruagaire. I believe that is a hairdresser. Anyway, I will never forget the day when I asked her if she could cut Alluren's hair instead of mine; she turned to me, crossed her arms and pouted."

Huvnor crossed his arms and, trying to mimic Lily's expression, said in a childlike voice, "No, Daddy, you are more of a project."

Huvnor and Slaith laughed heartily, and Huvnor continued, "Thankfully, she was an oblivious child back then and didn't realise that I had given her a blunt scissors... Otherwise, I would have been bald if they were sharper!"

Slaith raised his eyebrow, smirking slightly. "Do you remember a time when you never wanted children?"

Huvnor nodded. "Yes, I remember. I was young and had never met a woman like Alluren before. I didn't know what love truly felt like, even though I thought I did. But as time passed, Alluren and I fell more deeply in love than ever, and we knew we wanted to start a family."

Huvnor scanned the area. "Did you see Alluren come back inside?"

Slaith's expression changed from relaxed to alert as he thought momentarily.

"No," Slaith mouthed, getting up from his seat.

Huvnor followed suit as they hurried towards the well.

"Alluren, Alluren!" Huvnor shouted, but there was no answer.

Their hearts pounding, they quickened their pace.

Approaching the well behind the hut, Slaith and Huvnor saw Alluren lying motionless on the ground.

Slaith quickly checked her pulse and let out a sigh of relief. "She's alive, just unconscious," he said to Huvnor.

Huvnor let out a grateful breath. "Thank God."

Slaith looked around the well and heard Alluren moaning softly.

Huvnor picked her up, carrying her back into the house and laying her on the couch.

Slaith followed, and Huvnor sat beside Alluren, waiting for her to wake up.

When Alluren finally regained consciousness, she cried in horror, "My baby, my poor baby! I couldn't save her. Why did she walk into the forest alone? Why?"

Huvnor rushed to her side, cradling her in his arms. "What do you mean? Our child is okay, fast asleep. Don't you remember putting her to bed? You just had a nightmare, that is all."

Alluren stared in terror behind Slaith as she attempted to stand up and shouted, "Run! That monster is behind you!"

Slaith quickly turned to look, but there was nothing there.

Slaith gently forced Alluren back onto the couch. "You are hallucinating. What happened after you left this room? Please try to remember. It's important."

Alluren stammered, "I... I remember walking to the well to get some water, and I got the bucket and put it in the well. Then I sat down briefly, drank some water, and collapsed to the ground. When I woke up, I heard our child's screams coming from the forest, and I ran towards the noise... and then I saw..."

Alluren's wails grew louder as she continued, "I saw our baby girl. I couldn't save her. I can't believe she's gone. My poor baby, my poor baby."

Huvnor hugged Alluren, trying to calm her down. "Everything is fine. She's alive. You just had a nightmare," he whispered.

Huvnor then looked at Slaith with concern.

Slaith quickly got his sword and said, "I need to go back to the well and figure out what happened."

Huvnor nodded briskly.

When Slaith got near the well, he looked around and smelled the bucket.

The water smelt strange, and inside the well, the water looked a lot darker than usual.

Slaith looked closer and saw fungi on the sides of the well.

The mushroom was a rare species which shouldn't have been there.

Slaith walked back into the hut to get a bottle.

Slaith poured the leftover tainted water into the bottle, closed the lid, and attached it to the side of his belt.

Slaith rushed back into the house and looked at Huvnor, who stared back, and Slaith signalled him to join him in the corner by tilting his head to the left.

Huvnor nodded and gently tucked Alluren under the covers of the couch as he got up slowly.

Huvnor then walked towards Slaith, who grabbed him by the shoulder and whispered, "We must leave here. It is not safe. I think someone poisoned her with some mushroom or other plant, but I don't know if it is fatal. So, now we must go to the botanist to get more information and find a cure."

Then, Loac walked into the room, saw Alluren lying on the couch, and looked straight at Slaith.

"Is Alluren okay?" Loac asked.

Slaith walked up to Loac, lowered himself, and grabbed Loac by the shoulders. "She is unwell, and we must bring her to the botanist. We need to leave now, so please gather your things."

Loac nodded silently and walked back to his room to gather his items.

Huvnor went into another room and returned with Lily in his hands.

When Loac walked into the room, Huvnor turned to Loac and said, "Can you grab my bags from over there on the left and put them in the hay wagon?"

Loac nodded, grabbed Huvnor's bag, and went to the hay wagon.

Loac left Huvnor's bag and returned to get his bag and put it in the hay wagon.

Slaith carefully lifted Alluren into his arms and placed her in the hay wagon.

Loac sat beside her while Huvnor and Lily took a seat.

Rex followed and jumped onto the hay wagon, sitting next to Huvnor and Lily.

Slaith mounted Sage and led the way towards the nearest town.

As they journeyed towards the nearest town, Huvnor's daughter was a dainty eleven-year-old girl with striking blue eyes cascading blonde hair.

Despite her age, she had a sweet, childlike appearance that made her seem younger than she was.

Lily turned to Alluren, lying unconscious on the hay wagon's wooden floor, and then looked back at her father. "What's wrong with Mother? Will she be okay?" she asked, her voice quivering as she sniffled.

Huvnor hugged Lily tightly and softly said, "Don't be sad. Your mother is just sleeping. We are taking her to the botanist, who will give her medicine to make her feel better. She'll be fine, my dear."

Lily then put her head on Huvnor's chest, and Loac looked at Lily, a sad sigh escaping his mouth.

Lily got even more upset and was on the verge of tears until Loac chimed in, "Come, sit next to me. Please, keep me company. I am awfully bored."

She nodded and crawled towards Loac.

Loac tried to lighten her mood in a cheerful tone. "Now, let's play a game."

Lily looked at Loac. "What type of game?"

Loac replied, "I am going to look around for an object, and you need to guess what object I chose. The only clue I'll give you is the first letter of the name of that object."

Lily smiled a little as she got ready for the game.

"Okay, I will go first." Loac looked around briefly and continued, "The first letter is T."

Lily looked around, exclaiming, "Is it a tree?"

Loac smiled. "You are a smart young lady. Yes, it is a tree, and it is your go."

Lily cheered up a bit and started looking around.

With her tiny hand lightly clenched at the side of her right chin, she thought hard and finally said, "The first letter is R."

Loac began guessing what it might be.

In the meantime, Slaith turned around to check on Huvnor and Alluren and saw Loac playing with Lily, trying to keep her occupied.

Slaith smiled and then turned back to focus on the journey ahead.

Chapter Eleven
The Oblivious Ally

As they arrived at the village of Vastam, Slaith pulled on the reins and brought Sage to a halt in front of a triangle-shaped inn where bright light seeped through the windows before them, and a warm orange blanket covered the sky.

Slaith dismounted Sage and turned to Huvnor, who was sitting on the hay wagon.

Slaith spoke, "It's best to take your child to a room in this inn. I will come back to you once I find out what happened. You have my word that I will take good care of Alluren."

Huvnor's concern was evident as he asked, "What about the boy?"

Slaith looked at Loac and replied, "He will come with me. You have enough to deal with your child, and she needs you. Loac and I will take care of Alluren."

Tears started to well up in Huvnor's eyes as he said, "Thank you. This will be another debt owed to you that I might never be able to repay."

Huvnor then got up from the hay wagon, lifted Lily and Rex and walked with them into the inn.

As Slaith watched Huvnor walk away, carrying Lily and Rex in his arms, he turned to Loac and said, "Come, boy, help me carry that bag over there."

Loac obeyed and picked up the bag, putting it over his left shoulder.

Slaith lifted Alluren and began towards the botanist's shop, with Loac following close behind.

The village was still a bustling place with an open landscape where the foothills of the low mountains lay near a vast ocean.

Slaith and Loac rushed through a narrow path separated by small stone walls, trying to avoid bashing the villagers who passed by as they looked for the botanist.

Eventually, Slaith called out to a nearby villager, "Excuse me, do you know where the botanists are located? We need to get there as soon as possible."

The stranger looked at Alluren in shock and quickly replied, "Yes, follow me!"

Slaith and Loac hurriedly followed the villager, struggling to keep up with his fast pace as they made their way to the end of the village; the aroma of fish and ocean scents filled the air as they rushed to where the herbal shop was located.

As they arrived, Slaith stormed into the small stone hut with Loac, desperately pleading with the botanist, "Please, you must help her now. We don't have time to wait."

The woman jumped with the panic Slaith's voice created and directed him. "Shh, I need to concentrate. Can you put her down over there? I will look at her soon, but you must understand that many patients need my help. I will do my best, but I can't make any promises."

Slaith pleaded, "Can you please look at her now? I will do anything to help you in any way I can if you can examine her right away."

The woman turned to face Slaith as her short, mid-length black hair brushed past her face and replied, "You will just have to wait. I'm sorry."

Her green eyes rested on Alluren's unconscious form, and her expression grew solemn.

She noticed Slaith's sword handle and sighed. "I'll attend to her only if you can provide the necessary supplies. Slaith, I've heard rumours about you. People call you a fiend, a snake, and a ruthless murderer. But I've also heard rumours you save people and helped them when they desperately needed it, and I hope the latter is true for everyone's sake."

She glanced at Alluren, Loac, Slaith, and the other patients before returning to Slaith.

"I haven't received any supplies for a few weeks, and I urgently need them. I should have received them a few days ago, but the merchant never arrived. That's unlike him, and I'm afraid something might have happened on his journey."

She sighed again, looked at the ground, and said, "I asked some villagers to find out what happened after I noticed the merchant never arrived, and unfortunately, I never saw those people again, too."

She turned to look at Slaith. "Can you please investigate what happened and try to gather my supplies? Once I receive the supplies, I will do my best to help this lady."

Slaith nodded. "Yes, I will get you those supplies. I will do my best. But can you please look at her now? Maybe there are supplies you will need to help her, and I can get them, too."

The botanist nodded, went over to Alluren, lifted her eyelids with leather gloves, and touched her forehead.

She contemplated. "She looks unconscious and has a fever. We need to reduce the fever before it gets worse."

She went to another corner, grabbed a cloth, and dipped it in cold water.

She rushed back to Alluren and put the fabric on her head.

The botanist turned to Slaith and asked. "Do you have any idea what caused it?"

"Yes," Slaith admitted as he passed the bottle to her.

Slaith continued, "I think she got poisoned. I saw pieces of fungi and other herbs in a well where she got the water from."

The botanist emptied the bottle into a bowl, smelled it, and picked up the fungi and herbs to inspect. "Yes, you are right. She certainly seems like she was poisoned, and if this is what I think, then I doubt she would last a week without help. She is fragile. Tell me how long she was showing symptoms."

Slaith shrugged. "Less than a day."

She nodded. "Hmmm…We don't have much time, but I need to examine her more to be sure, which will take a while."

Slaith nodded. "Thank you. I will look for your supplies if you tell me where the merchant comes from."

The botanist passed him a piece of parchment with a list of the supplies.

The botanist continued, "The merchant belongs to a village north of here. Just take the first right and follow the path with lesser grass."

"Thank you, Slaith. I would go myself, but I'm afraid something might happen to my patients while I am gone or worse, or something would happen to me, and there would be no one to look after the sick."

Slaith shook his head. "You should never venture out in the forest alone. You are required here urgently. I will go now, but can you please look after Loac?"

Loac rolled his eyes. "Slaith, I can help. And I want to help, Slaith. Please, let me come with you."

Slaith quickly turned to face Loac with a stern gaze, with suppressed anger in his voice, "You will stay here, boy. That is the end of it."

Slaith turned to look at the botanist a final time before he nodded swiftly and left the hut.

Loac turned around, sat on the chair with a thump, and mumbled mockingly, "Stay boy, do as you're told."

The anger boiled inside Loac until he couldn't take it anymore.

With a sudden burst of energy, he jumped off the chair and bolted out of the hut, leaving the botanist shouting his name and trying to stop him.

Loac ran as fast as he could, not stopping until he was sure he had put enough distance between himself and the botanist.

As Loac entered the main part of the village, he scanned his surroundings for any weapons he could use to defend himself.

After a while of aimless wandering, Loac's eyes fell on a gleaming sword hanging over the edge of a table at a merchant stall that sold weapons and armour.

Loac snatched the blade without a second thought and quickly hid it under his tunic, ensuring no one had seen him.

Loac then set off in the direction that Slaith had gone.

Slaith walked a few steps into the man-made path carved by people travelling.

Slaith couldn't help but notice a destroyed wagon in the distance in the middle of the path next to the forest.

Slaith saw something that made his blood run cold as he approached it.

Human remains with deep claw marks embedded into their bodies and bloody patches leading into the forest.

Despite the botanist's suggestion of ample supplies, only a few items were left in the hay wagon.

Slaith drew his sword and followed the blood trail that led deeper into the forest.

The rustling of the tree branches echoed around him, punctuated by the sudden flapping of birds' wings taking flight.

Slaith's foot hit an unexpected obstacle without warning, and he stared at yet another fallen body.

Slaith lowered himself to inspect it and noticed that the person had suffered a head injury from a blunt object.

Suddenly, Slaith heard a twig snap behind him and whirled around to see a heavily built man.

Before he could utter a word, a sharp pain shot through his head, and everything went dark.

Struggling to keep his vision clear, Slaith saw the man who had struck him with a log.

The next moment, he lay on the ground, the thieves rifling through his belongings.

It was all a blur for Slaith, but he tried his best to resist, only to find that he couldn't overpower the men kneeling on him.

One thief asked his companion, "What about him?"

The other replied, "Do nothing. Just knock him out again and leave him to the Draganther. Maybe we should tie him up."

The thief hit Slaith across the head, and everything again went dark.

Slaith's senses slowly returned to him, an icy breath exhaled deeply from his mouth as pitch black enveloped the forest and the sounds of crickets chirping away.

Tree branches rustled suddenly with a loud screech that echoed through the woods.

Slaith adjusted to the surroundings and saw a Draganther emerging from the trees.

It had a panther's body and a dragon's scales and wings.

The Draganther charged towards him.

Slaith tried to grab his sword but realised he was tied to a tree.

Slaith struggled, trying to break free, but to his despair, he was utterly defenceless, unable to move against the creature's approach.

As the Draganther moved closer, Slaith's heart raced with fear.

Slaith was completely vulnerable, and he couldn't find his sword anywhere.

With wide eyes, Slaith watched as the creature came closer and sniffed him, its jaws poised to bite into his neck.

Overcome with fear, Slaith closed his eyes, awaiting his fate.

The Draganther let out a loud screech, and Slaith felt something wet covering him.

When Slaith opened his eyes, he saw a sword had pierced the Draganther's body, and the creature fell, revealing Loac standing behind him, holding the bloody sword.

Slaith sighed in relief, but it was short-lived as Slaith realised what happened and yelled out, "What are you doing here? I told you to stay. You never listen to me, boy."

Loac rolled his eyes as he retorted, "Well, if I had listened to you, you would be dead right now."

Loac walked over to Slaith and cut the rope binding him to the tree, allowing him to stand up.

Slaith noticed the small sword in Loac's hand and said, "I'm not even going to bother asking where you got that sword from. I'll deal with you later. Did you see anyone here? I need to find these thieves. They took the botanist's supplies and my weapons."

Shrugging his shoulders, Loac replied, "No, I didn't. I just saw the creature."

Loac added, "Actually, I think I heard a man's voice coming from that direction."

Loac was pointing towards the north, which led deeper into the forest.

"What was that creature anyway?" Loac asked.

"It was a Draganther, a hybrid creature that's part dragon and part panther. It has a panther's sleek and agile body, which means it moves very fast. We are lucky to be alive," Slaith explained.

Taking Loac's sword, Slaith declared, "I'm going to keep this until I get mine back."

Without waiting for a response, Slaith headed in the direction Loac had given.

They saw a bonfire up in the hill, slowed down and crouched through the tall grass, getting close to the bonfire where they spotted the two men who had attacked Slaith.

The bandits sat beside the fire as the fire embers and smoke filled the air.

Loac whispered, "I have an idea. I'll hit one man across the head with that log over there, and you need to be near the other man and be ready to attack."

Slaith grunted in disagreement. "No. That's a terrible plan. I'll fight them. There are only two of them. Please, I beg you to stay here."

Slaith slowly crept towards one man while staying hidden in the grass.

Once Slaith was close enough, he threw a stone nearby to distract them.

As one man stood up to investigate, Slaith quickly hit him on the top of his head with the back of his sword.

The other man charged at Slaith, but he quickly dodged the attack and stunned the thief by hitting him on the side of his head with the hilt of his sword.

As the thief was confused, Slaith stabbed the thief with the sword, killing him.

Slaith dragged the other unconscious thief by his arm and tied him to a tree.

Slaith lowered himself while holding the bloody sword and tapped the thief on the side of his head with the tip of his blade until he woke up.

"Where are the supplies and weapons you stole from me and the merchant?" Slaith demanded.

The thief whimpered, "They're in the tent. Over there."

Slaith turned to Loac and said, "Boy, can you look in the tent?"

Loac nodded and went towards the tent.

Loac returned and informed Slaith, "Everything is there, Slaith."

Slaith got up, and the thief begged, "Please, untie me. I'll just run away."

Slaith smirked without looking at the thief. "Not a chance. You left me to be killed by that Draganther, so I'm doing the same to you."

Slaith grabbed the thief and ruffled his wrist, purposefully loosening the knot, and then Slaith and Loac walked towards the tent, gathered the supplies, and Slaith picked up his sword and put it back in its sheath and handed Loac the miniature sword.

Looking at Slaith with a smile, Loac said, "So... I can keep it. Yes! We make a good team, don't we, Slaith?"

Slaith gave him a stern gaze. "You were just lucky, that's all, boy. Don't get too cocky. It could be the end of you if you do."

Loac sighed. "Fine. But after this mess, will you train me so I can defend myself and be more helpful to you, Slaith?"

Slaith responded dismissively, "I don't need any help, especially from an inexperienced boy like yourself. You'll get in the way."

Loac snapped back, "That's not true. You would be dead or seriously injured if I hadn't intervened and killed that monster."

Slaith grunted and continued walking back to the village.

Loac followed him, sighing in resignation.

Chapter Twelve
The Invisible Bond

Once they reached the botanist's shop, their eyes widened as they saw Alluren even paler and muttering to herself.

Loac looked at the botanist in despair and asked, "She is getting worse, isn't she? Will she be okay now that you have got your supplies?"

The botanist turned to look at Loac and Slaith. "I'm not sure, dear. I haven't seen too many people like this. Maybe that is because they were the unlucky few who didn't have people to help them in the way you both are helping her. Anyway, I will need to give her the medicine now, and then we will wait to see if she gets better. There is nothing more we can do besides wait."

The botanist looked at Slaith this time. "You two must rest. You can't do anything right now. I will find you if that changes, but you both need rest."

Slaith nodded, then said, "I'll return in the morning, but please find me if you need anything. I mean, anything at all."

The botanist responded, "I promise."

As Slaith was about to walk away, he turned to the botanist. "What is your name, by the way?"

She smiled. "My name is Lovila."

Slaith smiled back with a slight nod. "I will see you in the morning, Lovila."

Slaith and Loac then went to the lodge in the middle of the village.

As they approached the Innkeeper, the Innkeeper greeted them, "Good morning. How can I help you today?"

Slaith replied, "I'd like to rent a room, and if anyone by the name of Huvnor or Lovila is looking for me, can you please direct them to my room? My name is Slaith."

Slaith reached into his pocket and placed some coins on the table.

The Innkeeper chuckled, "Ah, Slaith! Huvnor was indeed looking for you. He's in room number twenty-one, and your room is twenty-four. Here are your keys. Enjoy your stay."

Slaith nodded in appreciation. "Thank you."

As Slaith and Loac got to their room, Loac ran into it and jumped onto the bed.

It creaked loudly as Loac lay down on his back.

Loac then lifted himself on the bed while staring at Slaith.

Loac thought for a while and then slowly spoke, "Slaith, have..."

Loac paused and then continued. "Have you ever seen this before? Will she die?"

Loac continued. "Slaith, if she dies, can we please stay around them longer? I want to be there for Lily."

Slaith's heart sank as he sat down next to Loac. "Yes, we will be there for them, but first, we must do whatever we can to ensure that doesn't happen."

Slaith continued, "I will also need your help, Loac."

Loac's head sprung up in shock. "You need my help?"

Slaith sighed. "Yes, you saved me earlier today, and if you didn't, then Alluren would truly be gone, but now we have a chance to save her."

Slaith continued, "But you need to listen to me. When I tell you to do something, you do it and nothing else. Do you understand me... Loac?"

Loac nodded in agreement, and then a yawn escaped his mouth.

Slaith chuckled softly. "I think it is time you get some rest. I will visit Huvnor."

Loac nodded, laid down on the bed, and, turning to his side, quickly fell asleep.

Slaith stood up and left the room.

Slaith found the room where Huvnor was staying and shouted, "Huvnor, it is me, Slaith."

Huvnor opened the door in an instant.

Huvnor eyes were red and swollen, and he moved to the side to let Slaith in.

Slaith looked at Huvnor with a grave expression. "Alluren is with Lovila, the botanist who is looking after her. We can only wait now. I will revisit her in the morning."

Slaith continued, "I also told the Innkeeper to come find me if Lovila needs me, so if there are any developments, she knows how to find me. For now, we need to rest."

Slaith took leave from Huvnor, and before moving out of the room, Slaith glanced at Lily, who was fast asleep in the bed.

Slaith then looked at Huvnor and wished him good night before he left the room.

Once Slaith returned to his room, he took the sword carrier from his back and laid it on the ground next to his bed.

Slaith laid down on the comfortable mattress, and a sigh of relief mixed with tiredness escaped his throat before falling asleep.

Slaith woke up and saw Loac looking out the window as Slaith lifted himself out of the bed.

Loac turned around to face Slaith.

Slaith noticed that although Loac had just washed not too long ago, he still looked and smelled like he hadn't bathed in a week, wearing clothes covered in tears, blood, and mud.

The only clothes that Loac had were other spare clothes Elantren gave him.

Slaith sighed before softening and asking, "How are you feeling now, boy?"

Loac momentarily thought before answering, "I am feeling better, but I want to see Lily and Huvnor."

"Do you want to visit them now?" Slaith asked.

Loac nodded enthusiastically.

Slaith smirked and said, "We will go now, and then we need to get you some new clothes."

They both left the room and knocked on Huvnor and Lily's door.

Huvnor greeted Loac and Slaith at the door and stepped aside to let them in.

Loac immediately approached Lily and hugged her while Slaith sat on a nearby chair.

Huvnor joined him while sitting on the bed, looking more rested than the day before.

Slaith's expression was serious as he spoke, "I thought last night, why would someone target you and your family? I know you've done things before, but that was years ago. It makes no sense why they would hurt you now. Unless..."

Slaith paused, and Huvnor raised an eyebrow in response.

Slaith continued, "Unless they're targeting you because of me. I still have enemies who would want to hurt me, but I'm always careful and make sure I'm not followed. If that's the case, I'm sorry this happened to you because of me."

Slaith's body tensed as he spoke.

Huvnor consoled him, "Don't be sorry. We don't know why this happened, and you always visited us to bring food and supplies and to check on us. You can't be sorry for that."

Slaith looked at Huvnor determinedly. "We will find the person responsible and make them pay. I promise you that."

Slaith stood up and said, "Can you look after Loac for a few minutes while I visit Lovila to see how Alluren is doing?"

Huvnor nodded. "Yes, of course."

Slaith turned to walk out of the room and strode to Lovila's hut.

Once Slaith arrived at the hut, he opened the door and saw Alluren sleeping.

A surge of relief filled Slaith.

Then Slaith looked at Lovila with a smile. "How is she doing?"

Lovila replied, "She is weak, but okay for now. She will get better in a couple of days. All she needs is to rest. You and Loac did a great thing. You both saved her life by getting the medicine to me in time and bringing her here."

"Although," Lovila continued, "she won't be fully herself."

Slaith's senses came to an alert at once. "What do you mean?"

Lovila explained, "She will be a lot weaker and still might get some episodes like she did earlier, where she sees and hears things that aren't there."

Slaith lowered his head. "Oh! I see. Is there anything I can do?"

Lovila shook her head. "I'm afraid not. We've done all we can. All we can do now is let her rest and recover."

Lovila tried to console him a bit. "Well, she needs to stay here for a few days, and then she can go home."

Lovila then took Slaith's hand, causing his heart to skip a beat.

Slaith stared back at her with intensity.

Lovila said softly, "You don't know how much it means to me to get those supplies you gave me yesterday. Now, I can save so many people. I am truly grateful that you helped, and if you ever need my help, please visit me. Or at least, you can come even to say 'Hello,' won't you, Slaith?"

Slaith smiled. "Of course I will. Now, I must tell Loac and Huvnor the good news."

Bidding her farewell, Slaith strode out of the hut.

Slaith knocked on Huvnor's door, and Loac was the one who opened it.

Upon seeing Slaith, Loac smiled and let him inside.

Slaith smiled at Huvnor and said, "She will be okay. She needs to rest."

Loac shouted in excitement, "Yes!"

Slaith walked closer to Huvnor and whispered, "Although, she won't be fully herself. She will be weak and still experience episodes where she sees things that aren't real."

Huvnor sighed, "Well, at least she's alive. That's the best I can hope for."

Slaith sat on the chair and said, "You know you can't return to your home for some time, or at least until I know what happened. I must stop the person responsible because they could easily do it again, or worse."

Huvnor nodded and replied, "I was thinking the same. I'll stay here until she's better, and then I'll visit a friend who lives in a nearby town."

Huvnor asked, "So, what are your plans now, Slaith?"

Slaith replied, "Loac and I will go to your house to find out what happened. After that, we'll move to Olentius to train Loac. After that, I don't know, but I won't be back for a while."

Huvnor replied hushedly, "You know, Loac can stay with us. We'll look after him while you're away."

Slaith's gaze drifted to Loac and Lily.

Drawing a deep, weary breath, Slaith said, "I considered that, but you already have so much on your plate. Besides, Loac has a history of following me whenever I leave him behind. I don't think that will change, even though he is fond of your family. I'd feel more at ease knowing he's with me rather than risking him running off and encountering something—or someone—that might hurt him."

Huvnor nodded in understanding. "It makes sense. He's clearly at ease around you, probably because of the trust he's built since you saved him from Cruatan and cared for him ever since."

A wistful smile played on Slaith's lips. "I believe you're right. That's why I must bring him along and train him."

Slaith stood from the chair and said, "Anyway, we must get going. But before we leave, I want you to have this bag of coins. It should last a while, as you must look after your family."

Slaith passed the bag of coins to Huvnor, who nodded gratefully.

Slaith walked over to Lily and hugged her, bidding her goodbye.

Loac hugged her and said, "We'll see you again soon."

Lily waved goodbye as they left the lodge and headed to the market to gather food, clothes, and water.

After shopping, they went to the stables to get Sage, who was happily munching away on fresh hay.

Slaith patted Sage on the head and put items into Sage's saddlebag.

Since they had fewer supplies than yesterday, Slaith left the hay wagon in the village.

Loac and Slaith mounted Sage and then journeyed to Huvnor's hut.

CHAPTER THIRTEEN
The Hidden Stories

Arriving at Huvnor's and Alluren's hut, Slaith and Loac dismounted from their loyal steed, Sage.

As they pushed open the worn hut doors, the haunting echo of their creaking filled the air, with a chilling breeze sweeping past them.

Slaith turned towards Loac, his hand subtly guiding him towards a vacant stool, signalling for him to settle.

As Loac complied, the chair gave a soft creak under his weight, mirroring the sound as Slaith took the seat beside him.

"Loac, a poisonous mushroom, was hidden within the well that caused Alluren's illness." Slaith began an undertone of sorrow in his voice.

Slaith sighed deeply and continued, "I suspect this wasn't an accident. It's as if someone, or something, deliberately introduced those harmful fungi to inflict damage upon Huvnor and his family; I need to investigate the well."

Slaith swiftly got up and walked towards the well, and Loac followed Slaith.

They both reached the well while cricket's chirps filled the air with a gentle breeze, and Slaith lowered himself closer to the ground and looked at the grass for footprints.

Everything looked normal, but he knew something was out of place.

Slaith put his hand on the floor and pressed hard enough to retrieve a bit of the mud to smell it.

Loac stood next to Slaith, watching, remaining quiet as a mouse.

Loac eventually spoke out of curiosity. "What are you doing?"

Slaith replied while observing the ground, "I am observing by smelling and touching the ground, trying to see if I can find anything unusual that might explain what happened here."

"Oh, I see," Loac spoke in a low, quiet tone. "My father used to do things like that. In the days before we were attacked, he insisted he would show me how to track one last time so that if I ever lost my parents, I could always find my way back to them. That was his last wish to me."

Loac's voice trembled as he continued, "That last lesson was completely pointless as I never had a chance to lose them, and now they are gone."

Slaith slowly looked at Loac's sombre expression before turning his gaze back to the ground as he lowered his head and spoke softly, "Your father's lesson was not pointless; it's a much-needed survival skill that many people don't have, so he did the right thing to show you. I would have been killed if you didn't find me in time."

Slaith took a deep breath before continuing, "Now come here, Loac; maybe you might find something I can't."

Loac nodded, surveying the area around the well.

Loac spotted the horse's hoofprints and nearby human shoe prints in the mud. "Slaith, come over! I think I've found something."

Slaith walked over, saw the embedded prints, smiled, and placed his hand on Loac's shoulder while gazing into Loac's eyes.

"See, your father's lesson was not pointless."

Loac smiled sadly as Slaith said, "Now, let's follow the tracks."

Slaith and Loac mounted Sage and followed the tracks without wasting a breath.

They traversed the dense woodland until the abrupt brightness of the sun emerged, casting an intense glare that beamed directly into their eyes.

They squinted and discerned that the tracks concluded at the beginning of a cobblestone path in a town known as Biveraral.

"What now?" Loac asked Slaith.

Slaith shushed Loac. "Shh. We don't know who poisoned the water. It could be anyone, so we can't draw attention to ourselves. Do you understand?"

Loac nodded.

Slaith, ensuring Sage was secure by looping the reins around a nearby fence at the horse stables, Slaith led the way deeper into the heart of Biveraral, with Loac trailing closely behind.

Nestled beside a large lake, the town of Biveraral buzzed with vibrant activity.

As Slaith and Loac ventured further, the chatter of haggling townsfolk enveloped them and the enticing scent of goods on display.

They maintained their cautious demeanour, subtly observing passers-by without drawing unwarranted attention.

Their path took them through the bustling centre of town, teeming with a diverse array of markets lining the cobblestone streets.

Besides the market stalls, they could also see a variety of shops, including the rhythmic clanging of a blacksmith's forge, the enticing aroma wafting from a bakery, and an herbalist's shop with its display of various mystical concoctions.

Loac's belly rumbled, and they both realised it had been a long time since they had eaten and rested.

Slaith looked at Loac. "You need some rest?"

Loac replied, "Yes, please. I am exhausted and hungry. Can we get some food first?"

Slaith nodded, and they both ventured to a fish market that sold every fish one would think of, like salmon, sharks and even a giant goldfish.

Slaith asked the fish merchant, "Can I please get any fish you caught today?"

The merchant smiled. "Yes, Sir, that will be Mantalen," and passed Slaith the Mantalen.

It looked like a giant goldfish with whiskers on the side of its face, a shark-like tail, and big lips that were a faded yellow colour and about the size of Loac's torso.

Loac looked at Slaith and asked with his eyebrow raised, "Isn't that too big?"

Slaith smirked, turned to the merchant, and said, "Can we only have a half portion?"

The merchant nodded, cut up the fish, and gave Slaith the body part.

Slaith and Loac ventured to the middle of the town to find a table with wooden chairs.

As Slaith placed the fish down, he broke it in half, passed the second piece to Loac, and said, "Be careful not to eat the bones."

Loac rolled his eyes. "I know how to eat fish, but thanks for the advice."

Loac scoffed down the Mantalen, and after a few seconds, Loac spat it out and yelled, "That is disgusting."

Slaith burst into laughter. "Well, I can tell you've never had Mantalen before. After you have it a few times, it is nice. Now, eat it. You will have to get used to not eating food you like if you travel with me."

Loac sighed and finished eating the fish.

Once they were finished eating, they ventured over to the Lodge.

As they got to the counter, a short lady with brown medium-length hair and glasses peeking over her nose looked at them both. "Hi! How can...Well, I was going to ask how I can help you, but it is obvious that you need a room."

The woman turned to the key box at the far end of the room, grabbed the key, and handed it to Slaith.

She pointed her finger to the left. "The room on the far left."

"Thank you," said Slaith as he handed her the coins and walked to the room.

They noticed it was small and bare when they got to the room.

It had twin beds, a table next to the bed, and another chair next to the table.

Loac rushed past Slaith and jumped onto the bed.

Once he landed, he made a satisfying noise.

Slaith smiled and put his sword and bags next to the bed.

Slaith sat on the other bed and looked at Loac, who had already fallen asleep.

Slaith got up and walked over to Loac's bed.

Slaith took his shoes and socks off and put the blanket over him.

Slaith then walked into the bathroom to freshen up a little by taking a warm bath.

Once he was done, he wrote a note for Loac.

"I am just going to look around the town to see if I can find any answers. Please, don't leave this room."

-S

Slaith put the note next to the table and grabbed his sword. Hanging it on his back, he left the room.

Slaith decided to get armour and so ventured to the armourer stall.

This stall had rows of gleaming swords, axes, and shields of different makes and sizes.

The armour market had a range of metal and leather armour, from full suits of plate mail to lighter leather vests.

Slaith examined the swords before him, testing their weight and balance.

Slaith's eyes finally settled on one that stood out, and he eagerly snatched it up.

Surprised by how lightweight yet strong it felt in his hand, Slaith knew he had found his new sword.

Slaith examined his old sword and noticed it was severely damaged and blunt, so he inquired about the price to the armourer.

"How much for this?" Slaith asked the armourer.

"Fourteen coins," replied the armourer.

"Can you put the sword handle on it?" Slaith said as he passed the armourer his sword.

The armourer nodded. "Yes, it will be ready by morning."

As Slaith turned to leave, he caught sight of a miniature sword that would be more suitable for Loac, as Loac's current sword was too large and unwieldy for the boy.

Slaith also noticed a small shield that could be used for defence.

"How much for these?" Slaith asked, picking up the sword and shield.

"Sixty coins," replied the armourer.

Slaith handed over the coins and collected the newly purchased sword and shield, securing them on his back.

With his business concluded, Slaith set off towards the Inn.

The Inn room was dimly lit, with flickering torches casting long shadows on the walls.

A group of men were huddled around a large wooden table, laughing and drinking from a tankard of ale.

One of them, a drunken, burly man with a thick beard, slammed his flagon down on the table and let out a loud belch.

In the room's corner, a minstrel played a tune on his lute, his fingers deftly moving over the strings.

Slaith sat down near the drunken men who were loudly talking and shouting, spilling their ale all over the floor while banging their fists on the table.

The loud noise irritated Slaith, but he purposefully sat there, leaning against the wall, staring at them sternly, observing the drunken idiots and listening to their idiotic tales.

The drunken man said, "I hear some stranger in the village came with a young boy."

The drunken man continued, "I was told that we should keep an eye out for those people and make sure they don't go to see Velinius."

The drunken man got up with his tankard in his hand, looked around the room, and spilt more of his ale. "If I encounter the older stranger, I will ensure he runs away from the village as fast as possible."

Slaith stared at the drunken man with a smirk and watched them as they started to laugh and talk amongst themselves.

Some more women joined them, and then they talked about hunting and other uninteresting things.

You could see the women yawning, the fake smiles slipping off their faces when the men weren't looking.

Slaith's patience was running thin.

Slaith lifted himself from his seat, pretending to stumble over to the innkeeper as he asked for more ale, pretending that he needed the support of the wooden counter that stood before him.

Slaith received the ale and purposely spilt it all over one of the drunk men.

Then, Slaith stumbled over to the drunken man and lowered his sword in his cloak so that it would be hidden.

The drunk man immediately got furious and yelled.

The drunk man was about to throw a punch until Slaith interrupted him and said in a slurred voice, "I am very, very sorry. I didn't mean to spill my ale. I will make it up to you by buying your ale all night."

The drunken man smirked and gestured with his hand. "Thank you. Come sit."

Slaith nodded and sat at the table.

Slaith remained quiet until one man asked, "I haven't seen you before. Why are you here?"

Slaith replied, "I have been on the road for a while and will finally return home to see family. Nothing special."

The drunken man smiled and turned to listen to the rest of his men.

Slaith again fell silent while the other people in the group continued to chat until some time passed, and Slaith took the opportunity.

"So, I heard you talking about a stranger with a boy. By any chance, do you know why they are in the village looking for Velinius? Is there some reward for their capture? If yes, I would love to be part of it," Slaith grinned.

One of the men answered, "Yes, I know why they are looking for Velinius, but I am not telling you. I don't know who you are."

Slaith responded, "I can help you if that's okay. I heard terrible tales about them. You will need the extra help."

The drunken man turned to Slaith. "Why? What is in it for you? What do you want in return for your service?"

Slaith replied, "If you can get me medical supplies to heal any wounds I may get in my travels, that will be enough. Those supplies are scarce, and I can't find enough of them."

The drunken man cheered, "I accept. Now, I heard they came into the village looking for Velinius. I heard Velinius tried to kill them or maybe make them sick, and now the strangers are looking for her to take revenge."

Slaith asked, "Do you know why the Velinius attacked them, and what did she use to try to kill them?"

The drunken man shrugged. "I don't know why she did that. I hear those people who lived in the cabin were nice and kept to themselves, so I would be surprised if they were the main target."

The man continued, "I think she just wanted the stranger and the young boy dead, and they were just causalities."

The group guffawed loudly, finding it funny.

Slaith glared at them, clenched his fist until he couldn't hold it anymore, and slammed it against the table.

The people looked at him while slowly reaching for their swords.

Slaith grabbed his ale, got up, and did a slight bow while lifting his hands slightly.

"Apologies, I think it is time for me to go and sleep. Good night."

Slaith purposefully swayed and poorly whistled, trying to show that he was too drunk to be in his senses.

As Slaith turned the corner, he put the tankard down and started walking normally.

Slaith stared straight ahead as he hid in the forest tree's shadows, waiting for the men to leave the Inn.

An hour had passed when Slaith heard a loud noise and shouting from inside the Inn.

Judging by the sound, it was the same group of drunken men, and one of them was staggering around, trying to leave the Inn.

Suddenly, a voice boomed, "I need to take a piss. I'll see you all in the morning."

The other patrons waved farewell to the man as he drunkenly stumbled towards a nearby tree.

With cat-like reflexes, Slaith quietly followed the man and swiftly drew his sword, pressing it firmly against the man's neck. "Shh, be quiet, or I will slit your throat."

The drunken man nodded and remained quiet, and Slaith guided him towards his room once Slaith reached the outside.

Slaith tapped on the window a few times until, eventually, Loac woke up and opened it.

Slaith directed the drunken man to pass through the window, but first, Slaith whispered in his ear, "If you even think about crying for help or trying to harm the boy, you are going to wish I had killed you now. Do you understand?"

The drunk man nodded with tears coming down his face, and Slaith pushed him through the window and jumped in behind him.

Slaith grabbed the man, tied him to the chair, and closed the window and curtains.

Loac couldn't curb his thoughts anymore.

Loac was confused, scared, and excited all at the same time.

Loac finally asked, "Slaith, what is happening? Why did you not walk through the door?"

Loac continued to look from Slaith to the man's face and finally asked, "Who is this man?"

"I didn't want to get seen. This man knows who caused Alluren to be sick," Slaith explained.

"How do you know that?" Loac replied.

Slaith replied, "The men couldn't keep their mouths shut, and I heard him talking about us. He warned everyone to keep us away."

Slaith turned to the drunken man. "Now, will you tell us who this Velinius is? Why did she target us, and where is she now?"

The drunk man begged through the tears. "Please, don't hurt me. I don't know much at all. I swear."

He continued, "I was paid by some man with a hood and told to look for you. That is all."

Slaith's blood seemed to boil.

Slaith pushed the chair and grabbed the man by the neck, roaring, "That is a lie. You even mentioned that name earlier when babbling like an idiot."

The drunken man pleaded, "I wasn't lying. That is all I was told, and I was given coins when I agreed. But, you see, this man under his hooded cloak wore a particular armour. It is made by a special person who only makes this armour for Velinius and her men. So, I know it was Velinius who employed him."

"Where is this Velinius then?"

"She lives far, far north of here. Near a swamp past the Slanitus forest, I don't know the exact location." The drunken man whimpered, "Now, please let me go. I told you what I know."

Slaith hissed. "Don't tell anyone what happened, or I will come after you, and you'd wish you would have never squealed."

The man nodded, "I promise."

Slaith threw him towards the door, and the man ran out of the room.

"Do you think he will not tell anyone?" Loac chimed in.

Slaith laughed. "He definitely will tell someone, but he might wait until morning once he sobers up, as no one will believe him now. However, we will be gone by then."

Loac asked, "Okay. So, what is the plan now?"

Slaith replied, "We must go to see a friend of mine. His house is a place north of here, a safe place where we can rest, and I can train you and get supplies for our journey. We need to sleep, as we have a long day tomorrow."

Slaith got into his bed with the sword at his side and fell asleep.

Chapter Fourteen
Sword of the Unforgotten Memories

Loac woke up and dressed quickly before turning to Slaith and shaking his body to wake him up.

Slaith groggily opened his eyes as he gave Loac an icy glare.

After a few moments, Slaith adjusted his eyes to sunlight shining through the window.

Slaith begrudgingly got up, grunting as he gathered his bags and got ready.

They left their room and headed towards the food stalls to gather breakfast and water for their journey.

As they left, Slaith's eyes locked onto the drunken man from the previous night.

Slaith tightened his grip on his sword and glared at the man, which caused the man to tremble.

The man said nothing, simply staring back at Slaith with fear.

Slaith and Loac continued walking, but Slaith kept his eye on the man until he couldn't be seen anymore.

They finally arrived at the horse stall, where Sage was kept, and both patted Sage on the head.

One by one, they put the supplies in the saddle and went into the forest towards the town.

There was silence for a few minutes; the only sounds in the air were the wind blowing and birds chirping.

But Loac disrupted the silence, which Slaith enjoyed before Loac began talking. "Do you have any stories you want to tell me, Slaith? I want to hear them. Oh! Can you please tell me how you got that scar on your chest? Oh! No, wait. Did you drink too much ale last night?" Loac bubbled with excitement.

Slaith just stared at Loac with a gaze that pierced right through him.

Then, he turned his head to look straight at the road.

"Alright, I'll keep quiet," Loac responded.

A few minutes of peaceful silence had passed when Loac suddenly shouted, "Look! Look at the beautiful bird that's humming. It has a long, skinny beak. What is it, Slaith?"

Slaith spoke. "It is a hummingbird and a beautiful animal, but they are drawn to noise and will attack if they feel threatened. So, you better be quiet, boy. They like the taste of young boys' blood," Slaith said with a grin, hoping this would keep Loac quiet for at least another while.

"Oh no! I didn't know that...I will remain quiet."

Slaith sighed with relief and looked for somewhere they could rest.

Slaith started looking around and couldn't find any hills until he saw a goat, meaning a mountain could be nearby.

So Slaith directed Sage in the goat's direction, and eventually, after riding that way for a mile or so, he saw a mountain with a cave.

Slaith grunted when he noticed only a few goats and deer nearby.

Slaith looked at Loac. "We will check if that cave is safe to camp for the night, but we must leave first thing in the morning."

Loac nodded.

As they walked through the ominous entrance, the air turned heavy and dank, laden with cold, moist stone scent while stalactites hung above them.

Slaith jumped off the horse and looked at Loac.

Slaith put his index finger to his lip, so Loac nodded and remained quiet.

Slaith, while still holding the reins, guided the way through the cave while his other hand held his sword tightly as he listened carefully to his surroundings.

All Slaith could hear were the drips of water falling from the cave ceiling.

Suddenly, a stone that was very close to them appeared to move.

Slaith turned around quickly and swung his sword, swiping the thin air.

Loac burst out laughing. "What are you doing, Slaith? Are you trying to kill the air? We need it to breathe."

Slaith glared at Loac.

Slaith pointed his sword at the stone. "Something moved. We're not alone in here."

Slaith walked towards the stone and kicked it, revealing a small hole in the wall.

Slaith crouched down and peered inside the hole, trying to see what was hiding in the shadows.

Suddenly, a pair of glowing eyes appeared, staring back at him.

Slaith quickly drew his sword, but the creature that emerged was not what he expected.

It was a small, furry creature with a long tail and sharp teeth.

Slaith lowered his sword and chuckled. "It's just a rat."

Loac bent down to get a closer look at the rat. "It's cute!" he exclaimed.

Slaith rolled his eyes and continued walking through the cave, keeping his senses alert for any other surprises.

After a few minutes, they reached a large area with a small stream running through it.

Slaith nodded in approval. "This will do. We can camp here for the night."

Slaith spoke. "Let's gather wood and water from that stream. And boy, I have something significant for you."

Loac looked at Slaith with confusion as Slaith took out a small sword and shield from Sage's saddle.

Loac had butterflies in his stomach.

Slaith passed the sword to Loac. "Now, this is yours. I will show you how to use it effectively once we get to Olentius town, but I would like you to have it now just in case you need it. I hope you will not need it."

Loac looked at Slaith with wide eyes. "Thank you. I will keep it safe."

In the morning, they left the cave, emerging into the night.

The wind howled, and the forest was eerily silent.

The goats they had seen earlier were nowhere to be found.

Slaith stopped and gripped his sword, signalling for Loac to do the same.

They crept, listening for any sound that could give away danger.

As Loac was about to speak, Slaith shushed him.

Slaith advanced cautiously, scanning the forest for any sign of trouble.

A screeching noise coming from the left caught their attention.

Loac pointed it out, and they headed towards the sound, swords at the ready.

Loac noticed bloodstains on the leaves and tracks on the ground. "I remember these marks, Slaith," Loac said. "My dad showed me how to track them. It looks like something was dragged through the ground, and the tracks remained the same; whatever was dragged was probably already dead."

Slaith nodded. "I agree. And that is why we need to be careful."

They kept following the tracks until they reached the place where the dead remains of some deer were lying around.

The corpses had claw marks and bite marks.

"Hmm, strange. Why was the body left like that?" Loac asked, covering his nose and blocking the smell.

Slaith responded, "They must have killed it for—or... it is watching us?"

Suddenly, there was a loud screech, and Loac pushed Slaith out of the way just in time for Slaith to avoid the Wolagist attack.

The Wolagist bared its sharp teeth, emitting a piercing howl. It glared at Loac with intense blue eyes.

Loac was about to run after the Wolagist until Slaith shouted, "No!"

Loac looked at Slaith, paused, and finally listened to Slaith and stopped running towards the Wolagist.

The Wolagist swung at Slaith, hitting him and sending him flying into a tree.

Slaith retaliated with his sword, but it only made the Wolagist angrier.

It tried to attack Slaith again, but he dodged the attack and circled the Wolagist, waiting for the right moment to strike.

Loac watched in horror as the creature hit Slaith, sending him flying in another direction.

The Wolagist then turned its attention towards Loac, but Slaith quickly jumped on its back, driving his sword into its throat and severing its head.

The Wolagist fell to the ground, defeated.

Slaith fell to the ground because of exhaustion, and Loac walked over to Slaith and put his hand out to pick him up.

Slaith grabbed Loac's hand and said with a smirk, "Thanks. And thank you for listening for once."

Once they got back to the camp, Loac went to sleep.

While Slaith's gaze remained fixated on the dancing flames, his mind was awash with unspoken thoughts.

Slaith's fingers closed around the hilt of his sword; its handle was embedded with remembrances of those he once held dear.

Slaith traced the worn trinkets and baubles gently, each sparking a memory of a face, a laugh, a shared moment from a life no longer present.

Slaith revisited the painful void left by each loss, weaving through the tapestry of his past.

Slaith's gaze shifted then to Loac.

A silent plea rose within him, hoping against all odds that the young boy would be spared from the cruel hands of fate.

Slaith's heart had weathered the loss of many cherished souls, and the thought of losing another seemed too heavy a burden to bear.

Slaith got up, grabbed the water jug, and poured it on the fire to extinguish it.

Slaith then walked up to Sage, lying asleep on the ground.

Slaith patted his horse and put water next to it.

Slaith lay in the middle of the cave to keep watch and protect Loac from any danger.

He then fell asleep.

The sun rose and illuminated the cave, glowing warmly on everything around them.

Loac stirred from his slumber, only to be hit with a pungent smell and a gust of foul air.

Loac realised it wasn't a dream and leapt up, screaming in horror, startling Slaith and Sage.

Slaith immediately grabbed his sword.

However, Slaith quickly realised there was no threat when he saw only a curious goat sniffing at Loac's hair and face.

Loac wiped his face and tried to shoo the goat away, but it remained persistent, licking Loac's face and attempting to chew on Loac's hair.

Loac's patience wore thin, and he began to push the goat away, but it refused to budge until Loac stood up, and the goat scampered off.

Slaith laughed. "A goat is not afraid of you, which means nothing will be."

Slaith stopped laughing and spoke in a more serious tone. "You need to act more like a man than a helpless child, you know that. I will show you how in a few days. We should go now."

Loac and Slaith gathered up their things.

After packing everything, they put all of it on Sage's saddle and went on their way.

Loac asked Slaith, "Slaith, can you please tell me about your sword's pommel? Why have you kept random parts of objects melted on it?"

Slaith sighed. "I was wondering when you'd ask me that. Fine, I will tell you. One object you will see is the top of a paintbrush. Do you remember I told you about a lady who was my wife? I loved her dearly and would give anything to hold her one last time. I might add that she was a painter..."

Loac interrupted, "Was she a skilled painter?"

Slaith replied, "Does her skill matter? What was important to me was her passion for it. She would sit outside for hours, deeply engrossed in painting nature. It brought her immense joy; seeing her that happy always warmed my heart. I would often grab my stool, sit beside her silently, and look at nature with her. We would laugh and enjoy each other's company without saying a word. Those are the times I remember the most, and that's why I carry the top of a paintbrush as a reminder of those cherished memories."

Slaith continued, "The other object you may see is part of a scissor handle. Can you guess why, Loac?"

Loac shook his head, leaning forward with wide eyes, and remained silent, listening to Slaith.

Slaith continued, "There was this man I heard screaming 'Go away.' I went to check why he was screaming, and I saw a bunch of bandits attacking the man who probably would have killed him once they had their fun. So, I jumped off Sage and rushed to the man. I got in front of the man and took the attack, but with rage burning inside me that grew, I fought hard. I ended up killing one bandit and wounding the rest of them, so the cowards just ran, and once they were gone, I fell to the ground and was unconscious. I probably wouldn't have survived the night without that man help who I saved."

Slaith looked at Loac, trying to get his attention. "You see, I woke up only a few times, and I could see the man struggling to get me on the hay wagon, but he did it somehow. I saw him forcing me to drink water and clean my wounds, and then he brought me to his home with his wife. They cared for my wounds, gave me medicine, and looked after me until I was ready to go."

Slaith exhaled deeply. "I took the scissors to remind myself that there are good people in the world. Like that man who could have left me to die and robbed me, which someone would have done, but he helped this stranger he knew nothing about. It was an enormous risk; those bandits could have returned anytime to finish their job. He knew if he didn't help me, I would certainly die. During the time they cared for me, I saw them taking care of other people who were very sick. The wife would even go to the town to give medicines to the clinic that were low on supplies."

Loac had been caught up with the story, and he interrupted, "Where are they now? Did they die?"

Slaith sighed. "Yes, they died because I was no longer there. The bandits wanted their supplies and hated that they lost to one man. So, they waited until I was gone, killed the couple, and robbed them. But I eventually found those bandits and made them pay, and so many people suffered because the couple was no longer alive to care for the wounded."

Slaith pointed to a unique thing on the pommel. "Another trinket you might see here is part of a soldier figure toy."

Loac nodded.

Slaith began again. "Well, I went to this town when I was living with my wife, and this town was the closest place to us. I would visit it regularly to get supplies, and every single time I came to this town, there would be the young boy who reminded me of you. He was always energetic, wanted to see people, and couldn't keep his mount shut. Well, he came up to me the first time asking for coins because he so desperately wanted this book, but he didn't want to ask his parents because they didn't have much and wouldn't have been able to afford it. He said they would feel bad or buy it for him and not eat for days, or at least that was what the young boy told me. So, I gave him some coins, and he said 'thank you' and ran off excitedly. I saw him again when I returned to the village, and he ran up to me excitedly and said, 'Thank you, mister. I got the book. I read it repeatedly, and I know it by heart. Can I read you a part?' I told him 'No,' but that I was happy the coins helped, and ever since that day, the boy would come up to me to tell me about his day, and he gave me that toy as a 'thank you.'"

Slaith sighed. "Well, one day, I didn't see him, and I got concerned and heard a scream, and I ran. But unfortunately, the boy was killed by a Griffin, after which I'd done the same to it."

Slaith continued, "To be honest, that boy is one of the reasons I kept visiting your village. I heard about the creatures there and the children going missing. So, I stayed close to prevent further incidents. I watched over you and the other children, mainly because you reminded me so much of him—eager, carefree, and perhaps too trusting. I couldn't bear the thought of another child facing the same tragic fate."

Slaith continued, "So, this is why I need to train you to prepare you just in case I am not around anymore, as I fear that something could happen to you."

Loac interjected, "I am so sorry, Slaith. And I understand why you don't talk much now."

Chapter Fifteen
Misguided Trainwreck

They finally got to the town called Olentius.

As they approached the village, Slaith and Loac were immediately struck by the quietness of it all.

The buildings were taller and wider here, with intricate carvings and designs etched into the walls.

But despite their size and grandeur, most doors were locked tight.

This was a town that was not meant for outsiders.

The locals moved about their business purposefully, rarely glancing at the strangers passing through.

Slaith and Loac felt like intruders, unwanted guests in a place not meant for them.

The streets were wide and clean but empty of people.

It was as if the entire town had retreated into the shadows, leaving the travellers to fend for themselves.

The silence was eerie, broken only by the occasional sound of a horse's hooves or a door creaking open.

The buildings were crafted from sturdy stone and intricate woodwork, with colourful stained-glass windows and carved pillars.

As Slaith led them to the most prominent house in the town, Loac couldn't help but admire the grandeur of the building.

It stood tall, with four floors, and was not attached to any other house, giving it an air of exclusivity.

Once they got near the house, Slaith jumped off Sage and brought Sage to the horse stall, and Loac followed him as they walked towards that big house.

Slaith knocked on the door twice, then once more and two more times, almost like it was a secret code.

The door creaked, and half of a man's face was peeking through the door.

The man shouted, "What do you want?"

Slaith replied softly, "I want to see you. Do you not remember me?"

The man looked at Slaith and opened the door, yelling, "Of course, I remember you. I apologise. I saw the young boy and feared you were a thief or something. Oh! Come, come."

The man was bald, of a muscular build, with a few scars that looked old and had healed over the years.

He was dressed in finely tailored clothes that suited the house's grandeur.

He wore a long, deep, rich coat with gold buttons down the front.

He spoke in a smooth, sophisticated voice, with impeccable manners and a polite demeanour.

The man gestured for them to enter the room and asked them to sit down.

They found themselves in a spacious common area as they entered the house.

The room was illuminated by several chandeliers hanging from the ceiling, casting a warm glow throughout the space.

The walls were adorned with paintings and tapestries of various sizes, depicting scenes of battles, landscapes, and portraits of notable figures.

There were several comfortable sofas and armchairs arranged in small groups.

In the centre of the room was a gigantic fireplace, crackling with a warm fire and emitting a pleasant smell of burning wood.

The floor was made of polished hardwood, with a few decorative rugs placed strategically to add a touch of colour to the room.

A large staircase made of marble led to the house's upper floors, and a few doorways led to different rooms on the ground floor.

Overall, the common area exuded an air of sophistication and luxury.

The man offered them some cheese and ale and asked Slaith, "Can the boy have some..." while lifting the jug of ale.

Slaith exclaimed, "Why not?"

Loac took a sip of the ale and immediately spat it out, grunting, "That tastes horrible!"

They both laughed.

Loac didn't respond and pushed the drink away.

Slaith asked, "Atalon, what happened here? This town was always full of life and many people walking around, but now it looks like people are scared to leave their houses."

Atalon began explaining, "Yes, this place was once a haven. It was full of life, but we kept getting these strangers into town. At first, they were fine. But then they started causing trouble, like a few bar fights. They kept coming back and started robbing people, taking everything they owned, hurting the people, or even killing them. I scared them away whenever possible, but sometimes I was outnumbered and barely survived myself."

Atalon continued, "So after that, the townspeople are scared and don't trust strangers. People stay indoors most of the time like a hermit. This is why they are afraid of you, and you also have a terrible reputation, so that adds on, you know."

Slaith grunted, "I know too well I am never welcome at most places I visit."

Slaith drank deeply from the cup of ale.

Atalon sighed. "When there wasn't any bandit, it would be a monster, wild dogs, or a wolf coming into our town. We had so much trouble that we hired highly skilled people like yourself to eliminate intruders, but we could only keep them at bay for a time."

Atalon gulped a mouthful of ale and said, "Slaith, I have an idea. Please stay here for a while. I will feed you like a king, and you will have an entire floor to yourself."

Slaith breathed out, "I can't stay for long. I have matters to attend to, and I came not only to see my good old friend, but also because I need your help to train the boy, Loac. We need to go past the forest of Slanitus. It has many dangerous creatures, and I must prepare the boy."

Atalon nodded, "Okay, Slaith. I will give you another offer. I will help train the boy to give you a place to sleep and food to eat, and in return, you will need to help me scare off intruders and get rid of any monster that will threaten our town for some time until we get the town back to the way it was before."

Atalon gazed deeply into Slaith's eyes and asked, "You agree, Slaith?"

Slaith thought momentarily and replied, "I will do that until the boy's training is done. By then, the threats should be gone, too."

Atalon smiled. "Great! Let's drink, and I will start the training with him tomorrow."

Loac had been patient for too long and couldn't help interrupting. "Why won't you train me, Slaith?"

Slaith turned towards Loac and tried to soften his voice. "I wouldn't have the patience, and besides, this man is a much better trainer and will help you far more than I can. Okay? Now, Loac, I think it's time for you to sleep."

Loac nodded as he yawned and went to bed.

Slaith turned to Atalon. "I need to get some much-needed rest."

Atalon nodded, and the old friends bid each other goodbye, happy with their agreement.

In the morning, Atalon gently knocked on Loac's door. "Come, boy. It is time to get up and get ready for your training."

Loac yawned as he slowly adjusted his eyes as sunlight seeped through the window. "Where is Slaith?"

Atalon chuckled. "He is still sleeping. Let's let him sleep, as it seems like he needs it. Now come, boy."

Loac slowly got off the bed and grabbed his clothes.

Loac went to the bathroom to get ready, and on his return, Loac saw that Atalon was equipped with a wooden sword and some armour perfectly fitted for Loac.

Loac scratched his head. "Why do I have to put the armour on? Is that even for me? I thought we were only training."

Atalon laughed. "That's my point. You see, you will need to get used to wearing the armour as it is heavy, and you need to get used to fighting with that extra weight."

Atalon continued, "This is the armour I wore when I was your age. You will get used to wearing it after a while, and you never know; it may save your life one day, so I want you to have it as I do not need it anymore."

Loac nodded, and Atalon passed the armour to him.

They walked into the training hall.

Atalon held out the wooden sword's pommel and pointed it towards Loac, who approached and grabbed it from him.

Without warning, Atalon charged at Loac, who was caught off guard and fell to the ground.

Annoyed, Loac grumbled, "What are you doing? I wasn't ready."

Atalon laughed. "Exactly. You always need to be prepared for an attack. Do you think your enemies will wait until you're ready to strike? No, they'll take the first opportunity they get."

Atalon ordered Loac to stand up and then began to circle him.

Suddenly, Atalon charged at Loac again, but this time, Loac managed to block the attack with his sword.

Feeling confident, Loac smiled, but Atalon swiftly parried his sword and pressed it against Loac's chest.

Atalon shouted, "I told you not to be distracted. Your enemies will exploit weakness, so you must be alert and ready."

Loac charged at Atalon again, swinging his sword wildly, but Atalon quickly blocked every move and parried Loac's sword again.

Atalon then performed a leg sweep, causing Loac to fall to the ground, and pointed his sword at him.

"Now I know your level, and there's much to teach you," Atalon said with a grin.

Slaith walked in, and his eyes fell upon Loac and Atalon.

Atalon called Slaith over. "You must be prepared to stay here for a while. Loac is nowhere ready and has a lot to learn."

Slaith nodded and walked to the end of the hall.

Slaith leaned on the wall, overseeing them both while they trained.

They took a break, and Loac sat in the corner to rest.

Atalon passed the water to Loac, who pushed it away and said, "I don't need it."

Atalon insisted, so Loac drank the water.

Atalon picked Loac up and tried to be a little gentler this time.

Atalon asked, "Show me how you swing your sword."

Loac swung his sword awkwardly, using only his right hand, but Atalon deftly parried Loac's attack with ease.

Loac's grip on his sword loosened, and it slipped out of his hand, clattering to the ground.

Atalon laughed. "Now, pick it up."

Loac stepped forward to retrieve his fallen sword, but as he neared it, Atalon swiftly executed a front kick, knocking Loac off his feet and sending him tumbling to the ground.

Atalon chuckled and remarked, "Remember, Loac, never let your guard down, not even for a moment."

Atalon shouted, "Loac, always be aware of the possibility of an attack. And remember, not everyone is truthful, so don't let your guard down too easily."

Stepping away from the sword, Atalon gave Loac a chance to retrieve it and stand up.

"That's good, boy. You waited for the right moment to retrieve your sword," Atalon praised.

"Now, come here, Loac. I want you to follow my movements and emulate my technique," Atalon commanded.

Loac positioned himself behind Atalon and mirrored his movements, slowly improving his technique with each swing of the sword.

Gradually, Loac's swordplay became more refined, his movements more fluid and precise.

Slaith watched from the corner, a small smile forming as he witnessed Loac's progress.

However, his smile faded as he realised how much the boy still had to learn.

Atalon gave Loac a pat on the back, signalling the end of their training session for the day. "Well done, Loac. That's enough for today. Let's go get some food," Atalon said with a smile.

Loac nodded and left the training hall to freshen up.

Once Loac was out of earshot, Slaith approached Atalon.

"He's improving, but there's still a long way to go," Atalon remarked.

"Now that I've started training Loac, could I ask for your assistance?" Atalon inquired.

Slaith nodded. "Of course. What do you need me to do?"

Atalon paused, considering his response. "We were supposed to have supplies delivered a few days ago, but the person never arrived. Either something happened to him, or he lied to me, so please investigate and take care of it. We can't afford not to get those supplies."

Slaith agreed. "Yes, and I think it would be an excellent opportunity for Loac to accompany me. It will serve as good training for him. Besides, this task will be less dangerous than what lies ahead."

Atalon nodded. "But keep a close eye on him. He still has much to learn."

Slaith nodded in agreement.

Slaith observed Loac wincing in pain while removing his armour.

Upon closer inspection, Slaith noticed some scratch marks and a bruise on Loac's face.

After Loac finished taking off his armour, he headed to the kitchen where Atalon had already prepared their food.

Loac dug into his meal, consumed by hunger, unaware of Slaith's presence until he spoke up.

Slaith broke the silence. "You know, Atalon is only being this tough because he needs to be. People or creatures are ruthless, so you need to be prepared."

"I know that," Loac responded without looking at Slaith. "I just wish I could be better."

Slaith remained quiet for a second before responding. "Once you have eaten and rested, I need you to help me with a task that Atalon has given me."

Loac's eyes lit up. "What is it?"

Slaith answered, "I need you to accompany me to find out what happened to Atalon's delivery man, as his supplies are running low."

Loac, overcome with excitement, jumped off the stool. "Can we go now?"

"Not now. We both need to rest." Accepting this, Loac went into the bedroom.

In the afternoon, Slaith knocked on Loac's bedroom door and said, "Wake up. It is time."

Loac opened his eyes and rubbed them.

Loac yawned, stretched, got out of bed, and changed.

Loac swiftly gathered his sword and shield and followed Slaith as they made their way to Sage.

Once they arrived, they mounted the horse and set off towards the town where the missing merchant was supposed to come from.

CHAPTER SIXTEEN
The Forsaken Thieves

As they arrived, they tied up Sage's reins at a nearby horse stall and quickly approached the shop where the goods were being kept.

Slaith wasted no time in addressing the merchant. "We were expecting a delivery from your store about a week ago, but it never arrived. Do you know why that happened?"

The merchant looked at Slaith curiously and asked, "Where are you from?"

Slaith smiled and responded, "We are from Olentius."

The merchant's expression turned grave. "Oh, I see. The merchant who was supposed to deliver your goods never came back to this shop. I was getting worried because that wasn't like him... I haven't seen him since."

Slaith let out a sigh. "That's unfortunate. Can you direct me to the route he normally takes?"

The merchant nodded sympathetically. "Yes, of course. He usually heads north from here and turns left at the crossroads. Just follow that path over there," he pointed towards the road.

As Slaith and Loac followed the tracks, they noticed that the cargo on the ground comprised worthless junk and supplies.

Loac looked at Slaith and asked, "So, I guess we're not dealing with monsters?"

Slaith drew his sword and replied, "No, it looks like we're dealing with thieves. Be on guard."

Loac nodded, drawing his sword as they continued down the path.

As they continued to follow the tracks, boisterous laughter grew louder and louder.

Eventually, they arrived at a clearing and witnessed a group of men huddled together, drinking and feasting on what they had stolen.

Among them was the exhausted merchant, tied up to a nearby tree, stripped down to his underwear, and with food smeared all over his face.

Loac's eyes widened in shock and disgust. "How could they do this to someone?"

Slaith's expression hardened as he assessed the situation. "These are no ordinary bandits. They're ruthless and heartless monsters."

Loac tightened his grip on his sword.

Loac proposed, "I have an idea."

Slaith grunted, but before Slaith could speak, Loac sprinted away and stopped when he saw the other bandits.

Loac pretended he didn't see them, but they saw him.

One drew their sword, and the other cried, "Get the boy!"

Loac ran away while Slaith snuck up to the other bandit and killed him before he could attack.

The leader ran out of his camp and lunged at Slaith, who dodged the attack and hit him across the head with the back of his sword.

Slaith then ran in Loac's direction with his heart pounding.

Once Slaith caught up to Loac, he found Loac crouched down, holding the shield above him, struggling to defend himself while the bandit kept swinging his sword at Loac's shield.

Slaith's heart was pounding in his chest as he shouted, "Hey!"

The bandit turned to look at Slaith for a moment, and in that moment, Loac thrust his sword into the bandit's stomach.

Blood gushed out as the bandit fell to the ground.

Slaith was shocked at Loac's bold move.

Loac collapsed onto the ground, exhausted from the struggle.

Slaith quickly rushed to Loac, sat beside him, and clasped his arm around him.

Slaith caressed Loac's face, his voice filled with panic. "What were you thinking? You could have easily got yourself killed. You can't just recklessly run into a fight like that."

Loac panted, "I'm sorry, Slaith. I will be more careful next time."

Slaith sighed and looked around the camp to gather supplies that might be useful.

Loac slowly walked over to the camp and collapsed beside the fire due to exhaustion.

Loac was staring at the merchant, who was still tied up.

Slaith returned to the camp, cooked meat in the fire, and sat beside Loac.

"What are we going to do with that person?" Loac said while staring at the merchant who was tied up.

Slaith responded, "I will untie him shortly."

Loac said excitedly, "Did you see what I did? I defended myself, and I killed the man."

Slaith glared at Loac. "You only killed him because he got distracted, nothing more. You could have easily got yourself killed."

Loac sighed. "Well, I defended myself until I saw the opportunity to attack, exactly how Atalon showed me."

Slaith grunted, "I was wrong to bring you here. You are not ready."

Slaith's body started to heat up as he shouted, "Get up, boy. Now."

Loac stared at him. "Why?"

Slaith continued to shout, "Just get up now and pick up your sword and shield now."

Loac reluctantly got up, picked up his gears, and walked towards Slaith.

Slaith suddenly charged at Loac.

Loac quickly lifted his shield to block Slaith's attacks, but his body trembled.

Slaith swung the sword against the shield like the bandits had done, but then rammed into Loac.

Loac lost his balance and fell to the ground, and Slaith stood over Loac angrily, putting his sword to Loac's throat.

Loac's body trembled some more as he cried.

Slaith shouted, "This could have been you earlier if that bandit could fight! This is exactly why I say you are not ready. I should have never brought you here. I made a mistake."

Slaith then lifted his sword and walked away angrily towards the merchant.

Loac lay on the ground for a few minutes while his body relaxed.

Loac got up and followed Slaith, but kept his distance.

Slaith took a deep breath before approaching the merchant.

Once Slaith got to the merchant, he bent down a little. "Were you the merchant that was supposed to deliver to Olentius?"

The merchant nodded. "Yes, yes. I was on my way when I got ambushed by those bandits."

"Good. Do you know what they did with your supplies?" asked Slaith.

The merchant replied, "Yes. I believe most are in the tent. Can you please release me?"

Slaith drew his sword to cut the ropes, and the merchant got up.

The merchant stared at Slaith, mouthing a quick "thank you," and ran away.

Slaith watched the merchant run away and eventually walked towards the tent, where he gathered the needed supplies.

Once done, Slaith shouted, "Loac, gather up your gear. We are leaving."

Loac grabbed his gear and started following Slaith but remained silent for the whole journey.

Finally, they got back to the house.

Slaith walked over to Atalon and handed him the supplies while Loac ran to his room.

Atalon just looked at Loac as he ran through, and then at Slaith.

Slaith was about to follow Loac, but the look on Atalon's face made him pause.

Slaith grunted in frustration and went off into another room.

Once Loac got to the room, he dropped his sword angrily on the ground and started throwing things around, shouting to himself, "I hate Slaith. I hate him. He doesn't believe in me like my father..."

Loac started to break down.

Atalon knocked on Loac's bedroom door and then opened it.

Loac quickly tried to pick himself up and wipe the tears away.

"Can I come in?" Atalon said in a soft tone.

Loac said, "If you like."

Atalon asked, "What's wrong?"

Loac spoke, avoiding the eyes of Atalon. "Nothing is wrong. I need to get better, that is all."

Atalon sat beside Loac on the bed and spoke calmly, "I know that is not the full story, and I understand you may not want to tell me because I am a stranger, but I am here if you do."

Atalon continued, "Slaith told me a bit of what happened to you in your village, Cruatan. I am truly sorry you had to go through that, especially at your age. Being around strangers constantly can't be easy, and I know Slaith isn't the best company."

Loac looked at Atalon this time. "I care for Slaith and appreciate him for saving me. He cared for me when he didn't have to, but I miss everyone I lost in my village. Most of all, my parents. I can't believe I can't talk to them anymore." Loac's tears reappeared in his eyes.

Atalon probed, "What did Slaith do to you for you to be so upset with him? I can tell by the way both of you came in. Usually, you are always side by side, but you came straight here this time."

Loac sniffled, "I killed a man after he attacked me, and I was talking about how good I was to Slaith, who got furious and shouted at me to grab my sword and shield, and he attacked me the same way as the bandit but knocked me to the ground."

Loac continued, "It scared me. I've never seen Slaith that angry before, and I wish he had my father's approach. Like my father would sit down with me and explain why I can't do things like that."

Atalon breathed heavily. "I understand your point. But you must understand it from Slaith's point of view. He has encountered the most dangerous people and monsters you could imagine. He has seen the best fighters die and has lost so much already. I know why he got so angry with you because he nearly lost you, and in his way, he wanted to show what could have happened...because he cares about you."

Atalon paused and continued, "I know what he did was wrong. But telling the details doesn't make you understand as much as showing would. All he meant to do was that, but he went too far."

Atalon stood up from the bed and touched Loac's shoulder slightly. "Anyway, I will leave you to rest and train you again in the morning."

Atalon went into the kitchen where Slaith was sitting drinking an ale.

Atalon sat next to Slaith and poured himself another cup of ale.

Atalon sipped on his cup. "You shouldn't be too hard on the boy, not yet anyway. I know why you were so harsh, because he needs to understand how easy it is to get killed, but I have only been teaching him for one day. He would understand more in a few weeks or even days with me training him, and he would be better at fighting. Then you can give him a tough love approach. He will be ready in time, but not now. You will scare him away more."

Slaith grunted but nodded and drank his ale.

Slaith then said, "Did you get the items you wanted?"

Atalon replied, "Yes, I got them. Thank you."

Slaith commented, "Good. What is my next task?"

Atalon sighed. "Yes, I have more work for you. Unfortunately, a group came into this town, threatening the people, especially a young couple."

Atalon continued, "Well, they harassed the woman, saying terrible things to the woman, and touching her inappropriately as well. The woman is so scared now that she barely leaves her house. Their poor young child rarely sees the outdoors anymore."

Atalon requested, "Can you please find those people responsible and teach them a lesson so they will never revisit my town? So that the young family can finally leave their house without fear?"

Slaith looked at Atalon and sighed. "Should I bring Loac? I nearly lost him, and I fear he is not ready, but I also know there will be dangers ahead. Those dangers are a lot worse than measly bandits. If he only listened and stayed near me, he would be fine, but he is headstrong, and I am worried."

Atalon put his hand on Slaith's shoulder. "You frightened the boy. I hope you know that, but your point was made even though the way you did it wasn't right. If he wants to go with you today, he will listen more. Don't force him to go. Let him decide on his own."

Slaith nodded. "I will talk to Loac after your training and let him decide if he is ready to go with me. Until then, I will give him his space."

Atalon commented, "I think that is for the best."

Slaith sighed and continued, "I remember when I was about Loac's age, and I was as reckless as he is now."

Slaith laughed. "I remembered when I climbed to the very top of a high tree, and I fell because I was stung by a bee. I could have broken my neck or something."

Slaith paused and began again, "Another time, I had something I thought was a great idea. I tried to swim to an island close to where I lived, but I would have drowned if it wasn't for the fishermen who saved me."

Slaith laughed. "I remembered him shouting at me, telling me how stupid I was. I wanted to jump off the boat many times to escape his nagging, but I was too exhausted, so I just stayed and took the abuse."

Slaith exhaled deeply. "I suppose Loac will be like me in a while even though he is not my own. I wish he was more careful and listened, but maybe he will in time."

Slaith got up, putting the ale down, and stumbled into his bedroom.

Slaith was too drunk to change his clothes, so he collapsed on the bed and fell fast asleep.

It was morning time, and Loac woke up.

Loac got out of bed, gathered his clothes, and went to the kitchen, where he saw Atalon.

Atalon had already prepared breakfast and gestured for Loac to sit and eat.

"Sit down and eat, Loac," Atalon said. "You have a busy day ahead of you."

Loac looked at Atalon in confusion. "What else do I have to do besides training with you?"

Atalon sat down next to Loac. "Well, Slaith wanted you to join him in the next task that I gave him."

"Did he say that? Yesterday, he made it clear that I wasn't ready," Loac commented.

Atalon replied, "You know what you did was reckless, and you could have got killed too."

Atalon paused. "Why did you decide to run away from Slaith and get one bandit to chase after you?"

Loac sighed. "I thought I was ready. I just wanted to show Slaith that I could fight and take care of myself so that I wouldn't be a burden to him anymore, and I wanted to make him proud."

Atalon responded, "You are only a burden because you don't listen to Slaith's words. You must trust him, listen to his advice, and follow his instructions in dangerous situations because he has your best interests in mind. If you are patient and learn from me and Slaith, you will become a great fighter like Slaith, or maybe even better. Do you understand?"

Loac nodded. "Yes, I do, and I will be more careful and listen to Slaith. But do you think I should go with Slaith today? Am I ready?"

Atalon said, "You should go only if you listen and obey Slaith during those dangerous times. If not, then you shouldn't go."

Loac smiled. "I will go then. When will we be having the training?"

Atalon replied, "After you eat your breakfast. Now, eat."

Loac finally looked at the breakfast he was given and smiled happily when he saw tomato soup and bread, his favourite food.

He gazed down at his food and started shoving it down his throat.

After Loac finished his meal, he asked Atalon, "So, what's the plan? What will you be teaching me today?"

Atalon responded, "I will be showing you how to swing your sword and attack you, and you will have to defend yourself."

Loac rolled his eyes and said sarcastically, "Oh, great. That again."

Loac looked down at the ground and sighed.

Atalon explained, "You need to learn how to defend yourself, but my approach differs from Slaith's. You will learn how to defend yourself better, and as you improve, I will challenge you more."

Atalon took a deep breath and said, "There is a difference between confidence and cocky. Confidence occurs when you have self-belief. One of the ways to gain confidence is by showing improvement, and that is what I am going to focus on. I will make you aware of your mistakes and show you how important it is that you don't make those mistakes again. But you will learn quickly, and you must. Knowing Slaith, he will not be willing to stay here for months. He is impatient, but I promise you will be a much different person and a better fighter when you leave this place only if you listen."

Atalon poured himself a cup of water. "Anyway, that is enough talking. Put your dishes into the sink and grab your gear. Meet me in the room that we trained in the other day."

Atalon chuckled. "I need you to wake Slaith up. He will be nicer to you than me. I recall when he was a devil upon being woken up, especially with me. Make sure you keep your distance."

Loac reacted, "Why?"

Atalon smirked. "Well, you will know soon enough."

Loac burst into Slaith's room without regard for Atalon's advice, scanning the room for something to wake him up.

Loac noticed a water bowl and seized it, flinging it over Slaith's face.

The sudden shock caused Slaith to lunge for his sword and swipe the air with it, narrowly missing Loac by an inch.

Loac's face drained of colour, his eyes wide with terror as Slaith glared at him.

It took a few moments, but eventually, Loac regained the colour in his cheeks.

Slaith apologised, "I'm sorry, Loac. I'm used to being attacked while caught asleep, so I reacted instinctively."

Loac caught his breath before explaining, "Atalon told me to wake you up. We must go to the training hall now, and then we will help Atalon with his task."

Slaith grumbled, "Right, I remember now."

Slaith rubbed his head, feeling a hangover coming on.

As Loac left the room, Slaith stared into the distance, the walls shifting around him.

Slaith groaned and muttered to himself in slight discomfort.

CHAPTER SEVENTEEN
Sorrows of the Stranger

S laith went over to the young couple's house to find more information.

When he arrived at the house, he knocked on the door.

There was no answer, and he hit again.

Still, he heard a noise like some item was dropped inside, and he grunted.

Slaith knocked on the door again and shouted, "I know you are in there. Atalon sent me to help with the people hassling you."

A few seconds later, the door opened, and a young lady with her hair in a bun, holding her baby, stood behind it.

She whispered, "Come in."

As Slaith walked into the house, the woman politely said, "I will be back in a moment."

She went to the room and put her baby down in the cradle.

Slaith looked around the room.

It was very bare. It just had a table, two stools, and a couch.

There was no wood in the fireplace and very few candles. This room was much barer than he would have thought for a family.

The lady walked in again. "Can I get you anything? We don't have much, but we can offer you some ale. Or would you like tea or coffee?"

Slaith nodded. "Tea, please."

Slaith looked towards the room where the baby was sleeping and asked, "Where is the father?"

The lady sighed sadly, her gaze moving to the floor. "Did Atalon not tell you?"

Slaith needed clarification. "Tell me what?"

The lady replied, "Well, he was killed not too long ago by those people you were talking about."

Slaith's heart sank.

The lady continued as her eyes pooled up. "He was trying to stop them from forcing themselves on me, and one man grabbed a bottle and flung it on his head, and he died instantly. The people ran off as they were shocked by what happened, but even so, that didn't last long. They started forcing their way into my home."

Slaith asked, "Is that why this place looks so empty? Is it because of them?"

The woman nodded. "Yes, it is. They keep coming here and taking anything valuable I have. Now that everything is gone, they take the only food that I have left."

She cried. "I am so worried. There will not be enough food. I would starve before letting my baby go hungry. Unfortunately, he is not old enough to eat solid foods, so I must eat. But I fear it is not enough for the child to grow up to be a healthy boy."

She wailed out of panic and grief.

Slaith was awkward momentarily, as he didn't know how to comfort her.

He asked, "Can you tell me where they are staying? Can you tell me anything about them so I can identify them from the crowd?"

The lady nodded and said, "Yes, they wear a brown hooded cloak, and the armour they wear has an 'X' mark in the middle."

She continued, "Last time, they stayed in the Lalran town. I hear them mentioning that town a lot."

Slaith nodded. "Thank you. I will see if I can find them and get them to leave you alone."

Slaith left the house and went back to Atalon's dwelling.

To Slaith's surprise, Loac and Atalon were both still training.

After some time, Loac rushed through the kitchen, breathing heavily and trembling.

Loac picked up a glass of water and collapsed on the chair, sighing in relief.

Atalon slowly walked into the kitchen.

Loac exhaled, "God! That was a very tiring training. I learned a lot, though."

Slaith hummed. "Well, you better rest for now, as I will need your help to deal with those bandits harassing the young lady and her baby. They killed her husband," Slaith said while glaring at Atalon.

Loac nodded. "I will go to bed for now to rest a bit. Can we go after dinner, as I am starving?"

Slaith nodded.

Loac went to his bedroom, and Slaith stared back at Atalon once he was gone.

Atalon shrugged. "Sorry. I forgot to tell you about the husband's death. But, honestly, I wasn't fully sure that he was dead. I never saw a body or heard about any funeral. All I know for certain is that she was harassed and rarely left her place, and I just assumed maybe that was why I had never seen her husband as he was hiding too."

Slaith commented, "Did you know bandits ransacked the house and took everything she had owned? She's even struggling for food."

Slaith moved closer to Atalon, still glaring at him.

Atalon was offended and tried to defend himself. "What are you implying, Slaith? That I knew all about this and did nothing. Of course not, Slaith. Do you think that lowly of me? That I would be so selfish to keep my food to myself?"

Slaith grunted, "Well, I find it hard to believe you didn't know her husband died after the fact you knew she was attacked, and you did nothing to scare those people away. Maybe that's because you're frightened too. This means you could be worried about your food supplies running low, so yes, I am accusing you of exactly that."

Slaith turned away from Atalon and sat on the stool, continuing, "But now that I am here, I will deal with the problem for you. You are lucky that the woman and child are alive. Otherwise, it would be on your conscience."

Slaith got up and rummaged through the kitchen cupboards.

He took food and water and started putting them out on the table.

Atalon interrupted, "Slaith, you can't take..."

Slaith glared, and Atalon didn't say another word.

Slaith continued to gather supplies, put them in a bag, and walk out of the house.

Once Slaith got to the woman's house, he knocked on the door. "It is me, Slaith."

The woman was looking through the side of the door, and Slaith handed the food to her.

Her eyes were watery again, and she smiled with pure joy. "Thank you, thank you, Sir!"

Slaith nodded and walked back to Atalon's house.

As Slaith entered the house, Atalon sounded annoyed. "Why did you do that? I need those supplies. I have three mouths to feed."

Slaith glared at Atalon, walked towards him, and said, "I knew it. You were keeping those supplies to yourself and letting that family starve."

Atalon retreated as Slaith got closer to him. "Well, not exactly that. I don't want to share. I have you and Loac to feed."

Slaith rolled his eyes and turned to walk to the bedroom to take a nap.

Loac was shaking Slaith eagerly, wearing his gear.

As Slaith opened his eyes a little, he realised Loac was in his training gear.

Instead of grabbing his sword, Slaith grunted, rubbed his eyes, and said hoarsely, "What do you want now?"

Loac eagerly replied, "Well, it is a good time for us to find those bandits and teach them a lesson."

"What time is it?" Slaith grumbled.

Loac replied, "It's nearly seven in the evening. Perfect time to survey and plan a course of action."

Slaith scratched his head, trying to understand what Loac had just said. "Why are you so eager and excited to find the bandits?"

Loac replied, "Well, I think it is exciting and will be fun!"

Slaith snapped, "It should never be fun. It is never easy to take a life or hurt someone, and it should only be done when truly necessary. Unfortunately, it is necessary that we stop those bandits as a lot more people have been hurt, and more people can get hurt or die if nothing is done. But hurting or killing should never be done for enjoyment. Do you understand me, boy?"

Loac looked shaken and stared at the ground. "Yes, I understand."

Slaith got out of bed and changed into warmer clothes.

He then grabbed his gear, and they both walked towards Sage and journeyed into the forest.

After some time, Slaith pulled Sage's reins, and the horse stopped.

Loac asked, "Why did we stop?"

Slaith put his finger to his lips, signalling for Loac to be quiet.

Slaith scanned the surrounding area, listening for any sounds.

Loac looked at him, eyebrows raised, and mouthed, 'Is everything OK?'

Slaith shook his head. "It's nothing. I thought I heard something, but it was probably just my imagination."

They continued their journey for a bit before Slaith stopped again.

"We'll make camp here for the night," Slaith said, guiding Sage to a nearby cave.

Loac was relieved to rest for the night and said, "I'm getting tired and hungry."

Slaith directed him to look for food while he prepared the fire.

Loac asked Slaith to show him how to make a fire, and Slaith sighed. "Alright, I'll show you. But observe because I won't be showing you again."

Slaith found two dry wood branches and a gigantic pile of dry moss that would serve as fuel.

Slaith used his sword to sharpen the top of one branch and placed the other on the ground, sitting on it to keep it steady.

Using the sword, he made a minor groove down the centre of the branch on the floor, which acted as a track to guide the other branch.

Then he used the sharpened top of the other branch and moved it up and down in the track, causing friction.

This created smoke, and eventually, a tiny ember appeared.

Slaith placed some coal onto the dry moss, loosely covering it over the coal to avoid the wind blowing it out.

As the smoke level increased, Slaith blew lightly into the moss, speeding up the process and creating a fire.

Slaith looked at Loac. "Now, you saw me make a fire. Off you go and get some food."

Loac nodded and went off.

It was a chilly day, and the sun went down, and it was getting dark, so Loac walked faster.

Loac saw there was a hill nearby.

So, he climbed to the top of the hill and walked to the edge for a better view.

Out of the corner of his eye, he saw a shadow, or at least that was what he thought he saw, and when he looked in that direction, there was nothing there other than plants, trees, and flowers.

Loac shook his head and looked around again.

Loac then saw a deer and moved closer to it, but every time he got near, the deer would hear him and run away.

Loac chased after it, but he never got too close and eventually fell to the ground from exhaustion.

"Get up, boy. And stop feeling sorry for yourself. You will never catch any food by lying down and complaining," Slaith said when he appeared behind Loac.

Loac protested, "I tried, Slaith. But the deer always know when I am near."

Slaith laughed. "Well, that might be because you walk like an elephant for your size. Everything can hear you. You need to crouch and move slowly, even if you are quiet. The fast movements would make you easier to see."

Loac sighed. "I suppose. But is there something that I could do to help?"

Slaith paused as he looked around, walked to a tree, broke off a few branches and twigs, and threw them at Loac.

Slaith ordered, "You carry them, boy."

"What is it for?" Loac asked.

"I will show you, but first, we must set up a trap," Slaith said as he returned with a box and some stale food.

Slaith put the box on the ground, put food inside, and used a stick to hold it up.

Loac looked at him, confused. "How on earth do you think the deer will fit in that box?"

Slaith rolled his eyes. "No, you idiot. I don't plan on catching something as big as the deer. Maybe a rabbit or something. Anyway, let's go back."

Loac and Slaith went back to the cave.

Loac brought Sage a bucket of water and hay and sat beside the fire opposite Slaith.

With a soft-spoken intensity, Loac looked into Slaith's eyes. "Slaith," he began, "we've spent all this time together, and yet when I truly think about it, I realise how little I know about you."

Slaith's lips twisted into a smirk as he retorted, "I could say the same about you, Loac."

Loac protested, "Not fair; I'm only fourteen. What interesting tales could I possibly have?"

Slaith chuckled lightly and invited, "Fine, so what would you like to know?"

With an eager beam, Loac unleashed his curiosity. "I want to understand your past better, Slaith. I want to know why you're constantly moving, why you don't have a place to call home, and why you never told me more about your wife."

Slaith exhaled softly, his gaze distant as memories stirred. While he spoke, Loac leaned in.

"You remember the tale I told you of the greedy king?" Slaith began, his voice a low murmur.

Loac nodded, his eyes widening in anticipation.

"Well," Slaith continued, "I grew up in that kingdom. I aspired to be the king's head swordsman when I was young. I trained relentlessly and could have likely achieved that dream. But that ambition was shattered when, as a squire, I was selected for a mission in the southern region of Xitamal with other knights and squires. Unfortunately, I fell ill and couldn't participate despite my sincere wish to do so."

Slaith's gaze dropped to the ground as he continued his tale. "When the men returned from the mission, they were exhausted, blood-stained, and their faces bore no joy. It was then that I learned the harsh truth of their journey. They had been sent to massacre the entire town simply for their inability to pay taxes to our kingdom. The king had disguised the true intent of the mission, painting the townsfolk as monstrous, but I had heard the truth from the man's lips."

Slaith paused for a second, then a tiny sigh escaped his lips as he continued, "After that day, my faith in the king and the gods was shattered, and my dreams of becoming a skilled swordsman had vanished. As I became more aware of the losses and tragedies around me as the days went on, I felt a dark cloud settling over me. I noticed the poverty, the starvation. Once clouded by dreams and aspirations, the grim reality of life had now opened my eyes. So, I abandoned that kingdom, aimless and slightly lost, embarking on a journey searching for a new home."

Slaith paused, his gaze still on the ground.

Then Slaith looked up, a wistful smile playing on his lips. "Eventually, I reached the Village of Laintif. Exhausted and famished from my journey, I sought the local food merchant. That's when I first saw her, my beloved wife. Her politeness, her captivating smile. I was drawn to her instantly, feeling emotions I'd never experienced. I started visiting her frequently under the pretence of needing food, though I think she saw through my lies swiftly," Slaith chuckled softly.

"As time went on, we grew closer. She wasn't just beautiful; she had a caring heart, which I loved the most about her. Those days were the happiest I'd ever known, and I found joy overshadowing my previous sorrow. But that happiness was snatched away when she was taken from me. Her loss was a pain I'd never known, leading me to live alone to become a nomad. I didn't want to risk feeling such profound loss again. I'm not sure I could bear it. So now, you know where I come from, about my wife, and why I don't have a home."

Loac's eyes mirrored the sadness in Slaith's tale, and he spoke softly, "I'm truly sorry, Slaith. I didn't know, but now I understand you better. Thank you for sharing your story with me."

Slaith nodded, a sad understanding passing between them.

The silence that followed was filled with shared grief, neither of them knowing what to say next.

Loac exhaled deeply before speaking, "I am sorry, Slaith, I didn't get any food. I should have been better. My father spent so much time showing me how to hunt and track, and I got so fed up that I didn't take it seriously. It is strange how things work out. Now I know why my father wanted me to learn. It was a survival skill, and I wished I took it seriously."

Slaith was listening to each word, but he was carving the stick, shaping the twigs to have sharp edges, and after a few were made, he got up and grabbed some wire from Sage's saddle.

Slaith tied the wire around the stick from one side to the other.

Once done, Slaith handed the handmade bow to Loac, who looked at it with a smile and exclaimed, "Nice! I have a bow and arrows."

Slaith said, "This should help with hunting once you know how to use it effectively. Don't get too near the animals. Once we get back, I will look for a better bow."

Loac started looking at the bow and arrow, stretching it out like he was about to shoot.

Suddenly, they heard a roar.

Slaith and Loac got up to their feet and saw a bear approaching.

Slaith drew his sword, ready to attack, until Loac cried, "Leave it alone! Please, Slaith... This must be the bear's home, and we intruded. Let's sneak past the bear and attack only if we must."

Slaith nodded, grabbing Sage by the reins and guiding Sage and Loac behind the rocks.

They slipped quietly past the bear without being attacked.

"Now what?" Loac's face went pale with the cold.

Slaith and Loac walked over to the trap and saw it was untouched.

Slaith said, "Let's go," as they hopped on Sage and headed to the bandit's camp.

After some time of travelling, they camped on another hill. Slaith showed Loac how to use the bow and aim.

Loac's first try was terrible.

Loac could barely hold the bow and the arrow while he pulled the string.

Loac struggled until, after many attempts of Slaith showing him how to do it correctly, Loac hit the target a few times.

After training was done, Loac fell asleep from exhaustion.

Slaith stayed up for a while, keeping an eye out to ensure they were safe, but, in the end, he fell asleep next to Sage with his sword by his side.

Once they were fully rested, they headed to the bandits' camp.

As they got closer, Slaith looked at Loac and the hill and said, "Go to that hill and have your bow ready if something's wrong."

Slaith continued, "I want to talk to these people first."

Loac nodded and went to the top of the hill as instructed.

Once Slaith saw Loac in position, Slaith walked towards the bandits with his arms raised, showing them that he wasn't holding his weapons but knowing they were within arm's reach.

When the bandits saw Slaith, they immediately drew their swords, and one spoke gruffly, "What do you want?"

Slaith answered, "I hear that you have been to Olentius. I want you to leave here and leave that town alone."

The bandits laughed loudly. "Why on earth would we do that? Just because you told us so."

Slaith gritted his teeth a little. "Yes, you should, before you all get hurt. I care for that town and the lady that you harassed. You all even killed her husband. I even thought about giving you this option rather than killing you immediately because I don't want more blood on my hands. It is a perfect option, and I think you should take it."

The bandit leader yelled, "We won't be going anywhere!"

Slaith, being distracted, didn't see the other man coming from his tent about to strike at Slaith with his sword, but the arrow that Loac shot distracted the bandit.

Slaith flashed a brief smile at Loac before unsheathing his sword.

One of the bandits lunged at him, but Slaith expertly dodged the attack by pivoting to the left and redirecting the bandit's sword to the ground.

As the sword clattered against the earth, the other bandit's sword fell from his grip.

Slaith swiftly turned and delivered a powerful strike to the second bandit's side, causing him to crumple in agony.

Loac saw that the other bandits were about to intervene, so he quickly shot another arrow, but it missed.

Loac didn't lose hope and shot another arrow, which hit one bandit in the leg.

The wounded bandit limped towards Loac, who shot yet another arrow, hitting the bandit again in the leg.

Finally, the bandit fell to the ground, unable to move.

Thrilled with his success, Loac climbed down the hill.

Slaith walked over to the bandit. "You should have taken my kind offer."

The bandit begged, "Apologies, I am sorry. We will leave the town as you asked if you allow us to go. You can have all our belongings."

Slaith grunted. "Why should I let you go after this? Besides, I will take all your stuff after you are dead."

Slaith raised his sword to do the final blow, but Loac interrupted, "No, that is enough. Let them go, Slaith."

Slaith grunted while lowering his sword and grabbed the man by his collar, lifting and shoving him forward. "Go before I change my mind."

The man nodded and ran away.

Loac and Slaith gathered the gear and headed back to the town faster than they did heading up.

Slaith seemed to be in a rush now, but Loac didn't care as he wanted to be in bed; he was desperately tired.

It was dark and quieter than usual when they got to the town.

They headed to the woman's house and knocked on the door.

The woman again peered through the door and sighed with relief when she saw Slaith.

She opened the door and let Slaith and Loac in, and just before she was about to open her mouth, Loac interrupted, "Well, the bandits are gone. They won't bother you anymore, and we brought you back some supplies."

Slaith picked up the food, drinks, clothes, and kitchenware and handed them to the woman. "We hope this will help you and your child."

The woman whispered, "Thank you."

As she tried to hand Slaith some jewellery, Slaith raised his arms away and shook his head. "No, you keep it. You have been through a lot. Use it to care for the child."

They left and returned to Atalon's home to rest for the night.

Chapter Eighteen
Dreaded Pursuits

Slaith, seated on a rustic wooden stool in the living area, was engrossed in deep thought.

The tranquillity was disturbed when the door creaked open, admitting Loac and Atalon.

Fresh from a training session, their lively chatter filled the room, yet as their gaze met Slaith's, their smiles faded instantly.

Slaith, slouched and weary, momentarily turned his attention to them before returning his gaze to the table.

The stools creaked against the wooden floor as Loac and Atalon took their places.

Loac broke the silence, his voice soft and concerned, "Is everything okay, Slaith?"

Slaith met Loac's gaze, sighed, and replied, "Yes, but we must depart soon. I've been trying to devise a safe route through the Slanitus forest, yet I can't find a secure way."

Slaith paused momentarily, then continued, "I don't know how to locate the Slanitus forest entrance. It's very well hidden, and I'm uncertain how to pass through it. Nonetheless, we must leave soon. "

As Slaith's gaze fell on Atalon, the latter broke his silence.

Atalon spoke, "I think I might be able to assist you in finding that elusive entrance to the Slanitus."

Atalon sighed, pausing before he added, "Although, I'm afraid you might not like it."

Slaith grunted and turned to face Atalon, his expression changing from sombre to interested as he focused on what Atalon had to say.

Atalon proceeded, "There's only one way to reach the Slanitus forest. You will need to know the chant of Kitoustis, the Egalitius call."

Loac interjected, "I've heard that name before. My father used to tell stories about a hidden forest far north of Cruatan. He mentioned that a witch was the only one who knew the path."

A smirk played at the corners of Atalon's mouth. "Indeed, you're correct, Loac. The witch is precisely why I suggested that Slaith might not like the plan."

Slaith and Loac turned to Atalon, their faces etched with curiosity as they simultaneously asked, "Why?"

Atalon chuckled lightly before continuing, "If you permit me to speak, I'll explain. The witch is known as Wyainalease. She alone knows the path to the forest, a knowledge gained from being entrapped within it by the person I believe you both are seeking."

Slaith edged closer, his attention piqued.

Atalon resumed, "However, Wyainalease is wary of strangers. Many who have ventured near her dwelling have either vanished without a trace or, if fortunate enough to return, come back missing a part of themselves. It could be a physical loss, a piece of their soul, or even a cherished facet of their personality. It's as if she strips them of their essence."

Both Loac and Slaith heaved a slight sigh.

Slaith lowered his gaze to the table, his thoughts deep and silent.

After a moment, Slaith looked up at Atalon with a hint of a smile. "You mentioned that she was trapped by the very person I seek. Perhaps, if fortune favours me and she listens to me, I could offer her freedom in exchange for passage through the forest."

Atalon's eyebrow quirked in interest as he responded in a curious tone, "Do you know how to free her?"

Slaith inhaled and admitted, "No, I don't. But perhaps she does. It's worth a try. We must discover why Alluren was poisoned to prevent this from happening again."

Atalon asked, "Isn't this journey potentially more dangerous than the poisoning itself?"

Slaith's eyes met Loac's, then turned back to Atalon.

With a nod, Slaith said, "Yes, it might be. But living in constant fear, suspecting everyone around us, isn't truly living either. I want to uncover the truth, stop the perpetrator, and regain peace."

Atalon nodded in understanding. "I see your point. I would likely do the same. So, when do you plan on leaving?"

"Tomorrow," Slaith announced, "Loac and I will depart then."

Atalon's smile transformed into a look of surprise. "Tomorrow? And Loac is joining you? Are you certain he's ready? I still need your assistance here."

Loac attempted to interrupt, but Atalon brushed past his interjection and reiterated, "I still need your help."

Slaith replied calmly, "The bandits who posed the real threat are gone. Over time, your people will regain their confidence, and you could spread the word to encourage merchants to revisit your town. As for Loac, I'll be there to protect him."

Slaith gave a slight smirk. "Besides, I'm not sure I could convince him to stay."

Loac nodded in agreement. "I'm going with Slaith."

Slaith continued, "You don't need me any longer. Moreover, I'm growing impatient and worry that if I delay, I'll lose my leads."

Atalon nodded. "Alright, then. Be sure to have a good meal tonight and rest well for the journey ahead."

They all shared a final meal before retiring for the night.

Come morning, Loac woke up bubbling with excitement.

He hopped out of bed, and gathered his gear.

Noticing Loac, Atalon called and handed him a bag filled with food and water. "Take this for your journey. Remember everything I've taught you, especially about listening and trusting Slaith."

Loac nodded in appreciation. "I will. Thank you for your guidance in my training. I need to focus on strategising rather than rushing into danger."

Loac added, "Now. Slaith and I can finally venture to that place and uncover what happened to Alluren."

"No problem, it's time for you to get going," Atalon urged.

Slaith joined them, placing a hand on Loac's shoulder.

Loac looked up and smiled at Slaith, who then turned to Atalon and said, "Thank you for training, Loac."

Interrupting Slaith, Atalon replied, "No thanks needed. I was happy to help. You both should get going now. I wish you safe travels."

Slaith nodded in acknowledgement.

Loac and Slaith then secured their belongings in Sage's saddlebag, ready to embark on their journey.

Underneath a moonless sky, Slaith and Loac found themselves enveloped in the profound quiet of the forest.

Only the intermittent chirping of unseen birds punctuated the weighty silence.

Their steeds' hooves clopped gently, an eerie rhythm in the otherwise still night.

Slaith and Loac were perched atop Sage.

Loac drew in a deep sigh before breaking the silence.

"Recently, I've found my thoughts drifting to my parents," Loac confessed, his voice barely more than a whisper.

"Every time I reflect on their absence, I feel like I should be overcome with sadness and crying. Yet, each time I think about my parents, I'm met with an unsettling numbness. I feel empty, as if my mind is frozen in a void of nothingness. I can't feel anything, and I don't know why."

Loac paused, letting the heavy silence hang for a moment before continuing, "There's a part of me that fantasises about returning to their open arms at the end of this journey."

Loac's voice trailed off.

Slaith looked down at Loac, staring at Loac, listening intently to every word Loac had to say.

Loac stopped speaking for a minute, turned his head to look at Slaith, and asked, "Have you ever felt this way? After you lost the loved ones, you told..."

Slaith locked eyes with Loac, his expression solemn. "Yes, I have. Everyone handles grief differently," Slaith began. "In this world, there is no book that tells us how to grieve. I believe it's a personal journey; everyone grieves in their own way. I believe there's no right or wrong way to do it."

With a softer tone, still gazing at Loac, Slaith continued, "I felt very much as you do now, stuck in a form of denial. I knew the truth, yet my heart refused to accept it. It was overwhelming. Grief consumed me to the point where I lost faith—in people, everything. I was trapped in a whirlwind of pain and anger. To avoid feeling such deep anguish, I distanced myself from others.

I'd push away or intimidate anyone who tried to get close to me. That's why I left and lived without a home, to be alone and to numb this unbearable pain."

Slaith lowered his head and exhaled an icy breath as he spoke. "I was quite cruel back then, willing to do anything to keep people at arm's length."

Loac turned to Slaith. "Did you kill anyone?"

In a gentle tone, Slaith replied, "No, I didn't kill anyone unless it was in self-defence. I was filled with rage and behaved that way for a long time until I met Veinaly. She saw past my anger and stood her ground against me. She was a strong woman who recognised my pain, like a cornered, injured wild dog that was afraid. I yelled and cursed, yet she persisted. She stood by my side, gradually peeling away layers of my pain. Over time, I opened up to her and others, but it all began because of her."

Loac interrupted, "I'm afraid of experiencing these feelings. I am afraid of what I may become. Will I be as angry as you were, or perhaps worse?"

Slaith answered, "We can't predict how you will grieve the loss of your family and everyone you know. But hear me now. As long as I'm here and care for you, I'll be there to guide you if you stray, just as Veinaly did for me."

Loac nodded, his heart filled with sadness.

Together, they continued their journey through the shadowy forest in companionable silence.

Twilight was setting in as they travelled through the eerie forest.

The gentle chirping of the birds abruptly transitioned into the shrill cries of hawks, as if sending a coded message amongst themselves.

Slaith's gaze flitted about the surroundings; the wind had taken on a chilling bite, and the forest's inhabitants hushed their sounds.

Further into the wilderness, more creatures emerged from the shadows.

A rabbit, poised to bolt, stayed frozen, its eyes locked on them.

Loac's hair stood up as he noted the abrupt sound shift and the creeping cold.

"Slaith," Loac whispered, "I feel like we're being watched."

Slaith responded in a hushed tone, "Yes, I believe we've been under surveillance for some time."

The sudden echo of a woman's cackle filled the air.

"Why are you here? Leave now, or face certain death," the voice taunted.

Slaith raised his voice, pulling the reins of his horse taut. "We mean no harm. Our path lies through the forest of Slanitus, and we hoped you could guide us. Perhaps we can assist you in return."

The woman's laughter rang louder. "How can you possibly help me?"

Slaith scanned the surroundings for signs of the woman, finding only the reflective eyes of the forest's inhabitants.

Slaith said, "Wyainalease, I believe you are trapped here, possibly by the one we seek. Despite potentially being foes, we share a common adversary. If you guide us through this forest, we may free you."

Wyainalease responded with a screech, "Only she who trapped me can set me free."

Slaith interrupted, "What do you have to lose? Guide us, and if we perish, you lose nothing. But if we survive, we could find a way to free you. If you kill us now, your imprisonment is guaranteed. However, aiding us might offer you a chance at freedom."

A moment of silence hung heavy in the air, broken by a low voice saying, "Fine, move forward and follow the animals. We shall meet soon."

The wind brushed against Slaith and Loac's faces.

They found the animals were still watching them closely.

Urging Sage to move forward as instructed, they noticed foxes, rabbits, and birds starting to trail in front of them, leading them deeper into the forest's heart.

They eventually arrived at a small, run-down stone hut with candlelight streaming through its cracked window.

The door creaked open to reveal the witch Wyainalease.

She had wavy black hair that fell over her shoulders. She wore a long cloak that combined the shades of purple and black, and her pale skin contrasted starkly against her dark blue eyes.

With a curt nod towards some stools, Wyainalease invited them to sit.

They complied, attentive to her every move.

"So," Wyainalease began, her tone acidic, "what do you want? Why do you seek this witch called Velinius?"

Slaith took a deep breath, explaining their predicament. "A friend of mine was poisoned, nearly killed. We suspect that she was behind it. We want to understand why she is after us, to stop her, so that we no longer need to look over our shoulders, waiting for the next attack."

Wyainalease grunted, "Fine. How do you plan to help me?"

Slaith sighed. "At the moment, I don't know. But I promise to lift your curse. To do so, you must tell us how you were trapped in the first place."

Wyainalease laughter rang hollow. "She caught me reading a forbidden book filled with dark spells, which she disapproved of. For my disobedience, she confined me here in this forest, ensuring I couldn't harm her. If you find that book, I can lift the curse. If I guide you, will you retrieve it?"

Slaith nodded. "Yes, I will."

Wyainalease whispered, pointing towards the forest. "Head far right. You'll begin to see owls and birds gathering. Listen for their low chirping. Repeat 'Val, Tatal, Arieach' five times, and you'll find your way."

Slaith asked, "How will I know it will work?"

Wyainalease smirked. "You'll know. Now go."

Without hesitating, Loac and Slaith left the hut and ventured in the direction Wyainalease instructed.

They started to see flocks of birds flying ahead and perching themselves on the trees and hooting.

Loac moaned, "I have a bad feeling about this. Are you sure this is the right way, and do you believe her?"

Slaith turned to Loac and spoke softly, "Of course. I don't believe her, and I don't trust her."

Loac interrupted, "Then why are we listening to her?"

Slaith continued, "She could have killed us, and, as I mentioned, we might help her, so I follow because it's in her self-interest to guide us the right way."

Loac groaned, "If you say so."

Slaith turned to look as he dismounted Sage and guided them through the dark woods.

As Slaith looked around, he couldn't help but notice that the forest trees were filled with birds, their chirping soft and low.

Slaith chanted, "Val, Tatal, arieach," five times over.

A loud screech pierced the sky, prompting Slaith to draw his sword and scan the skies.

Wings flapped, a breeze whipped around them, and a beam of moonlight bathed the forest.

A giant eagle like a luminous bird, resplendent in the moonlight, hovered before Slaith.

"Take me to the hidden forest," Slaith commanded. The bird soared into the air with a resonant screech and disappeared.

Loac looked confused. "How on earth are we supposed to follow that?"

Slaith pointed at the ground, smirking, where the feathers lay.

Loac's face brightened with understanding. "I get it. We follow the feathers. They will lead us to the forest."

Slaith nodded, leading them onwards, their path illuminated by the delicate feathers.

They left Sage behind as they rushed through the dark, dead forest with a cold breeze hitting their faces and the grass rustling beneath their boots.

Slaith came to an abrupt halt.

Slaith immediately felt his strength fading away and promptly surveyed his surroundings.

Slaith's eyes, though blurred, strained to pierce through the overwhelming darkness and silence around him.

A hefty gust of wind whooshed past, almost toppling Slaith over.

Slaith could make out a strangled, rasping breath amid the swirling sounds.

Swiftly turning towards the sound, Slaith's eyes widened when he saw Loac, his mouth agape, gasping as if fighting an unseen foe.

Slaith rushed over to Loac without hesitation.

Loac was gasping for air as if a gust of wind was being forced into his mouth.

However, the moment Slaith reached him, the gust disappeared.

Loac's coughing ceased as he opened his eyes and struggled to rise.

Slaith offered his hand, but Loac declined, insisting on standing up.

Slaith moved his arm around Loac for support, looking into his eyes, and asked worriedly, "Are you sure you're alright?"

Loac nodded weakly, whispering, "Yes, I am. What just happened?"

Slaith's gaze swept over the forest, seeking signs of the eerie wind, but it had vanished.

"I am not entirely sure," Slaith responded. "My best guess would be some dark magic, but I don't know."

Slaith turned his gaze back to Loac, concern evident in his eyes. "If you're not feeling well, we can turn back. I think we should."

But Loac was firm. "No, I am fine. Can we please continue?"

Slaith relented, letting his gaze wander over the forest again.

However, Loac's voice cut through the silence, "Actually, Slaith, I am not feeling too good..."

A groan interrupted Loac's words.

Chapter Nineteen
The Master's Sinister Pawn

Slaith looked in horror as he saw Loac collapse to the ground.

Slaith rushed to Loac's side, listening for Loac's heartbeat, which was weak but still present.

Loac's breathing was raspy and strained.

Swiftly, Slaith scooped up Loac in his arms, positioning him with his face towards the sky to aid his struggling breaths.

As Slaith sprinted back towards Wyainalease in the desperate hope that she might have a cure, his mind flooded with memories––the young boy killed and the caring couple who saved his life.

His vision blurred with painful images of his wife, their shared dreams of having a child, and then back to the unconscious Loac that Slaith held in his arms.

Slaith stumbled but quickly regained footing as Loac's coughing grew more severe.

Loac's breaths were shallow and infrequent; Slaith knew time was of the essence.

Slaith rushed into Wyainalease's hut, triggering memories of what he was like with Alluren in his arms.

Slaith looked at Loac, and the door slammed shut behind them, and the room filled with a disorienting smoky haze.

Slaith felt his strength fading, and before losing consciousness, he heard a whisper, "I'm sorry, Slaith…"

Slaith's eyes awoke from their induced slumber, and his vision turned from clouded to clear.

Swiftly, Slaith pulled himself upright, taking in the surrounding room.

A cold breeze, bearing the harsh bite of the night, meandered its way through the fractured window pane.

Frantically, Slaith looked around for his sword.

To his horror, it was nowhere to be found.

With a sudden burst of energy, Slaith launched himself out of bed and rushed out the door, only to see Wyainalease standing over Loac, chanting, "Afak Tin Nora, Alfak Tin Nora, hear my call."

Catching sight of Slaith charging toward Wyainalease, a wicked smirk twisted her lips.

With an effortless flick of her finger, a chilling enchantment took hold, and Slaith was frozen in his tracks, his heartbeat echoing hollowly in his chest as he helplessly watched Wyainalease at work.

Once Wyainalease finished chanting, she placed her hands on Loac and commanded, "Now take what is mine and set him free."

The candles that lit the room abruptly blew out, replaced by the terrifying sounds of the Wyainalease's screams and Loac's gasps for breath.

Then, an oppressive silence fell, broken only by the whispering wind and the rustling leaves beyond the room.

A gust of wind surged through the room, brushing against Slaith as the candles relit, revealing the unconscious witch sprawled atop Loac.

Struggling fiercely against his immobility, Slaith finally shouted, "What did you do to Loac?"

Slowly, Wyainalease lifted herself, locking her gaze onto Slaith before turning to Loac. "I saved him," she said.

Slaith hissed, "If you saved him, why can't I move?"

Staring at Loac, Wyainalease replied with a smirk, "I froze you because you would have interfered. I was mid-chant; Loac wouldn't have survived if you'd interrupted."

Slaith shouted back, his voice raw. "Then why did you knock me out if that's what you intended to do?"

Wyainalease's laughter echoed through the room. "You saw right through me. Yes, you're correct. I initially planned to take Loac to return him to Velinius for my freedom. But I knew she'd enslave Loac, and I'd remain her prisoner. So, I saved him, hoping you would help me."

Slaith retorted, "How can I trust you now?"

Wyainalease grinned, locking eyes with Slaith as she replied, "You've no choice."

Slaith grunted, "Fine. Now, will you release me?"

Wyainalease eyes fluttered closed, and Slaith, regaining his mobility, Slaith hastened to Loac's side, Slaith's hands trembling as he tenderly brushed the hair from Loac's face.

Loac groaned, his eyes fluttering open as Loac surveyed the surroundings. "Why are we here? What happened?"

Loac managed to croak out, his voice feeble.

Slaith exhaled a deep sigh of relief and looked at Loac with a smile as he spoke softly, "Don't worry about it. You're safe now. Get some rest, then we'll travel back to Huvnor and his family."

Loac tried to sit up as he spoke. "What do you mean? Stop. We are meant to find out what happened to Alluren, so we'd be safe."

Slaith insisted, "Rest. Just rest."

But Loac resisted. "No, we need to go. I'm okay. I swear. I'm okay."

Loac slid off the bed with effort, his legs buckling under him before he could stand fully upright.

"Please," Loac begged, "we've come so far. Can't we find another way?"

Slaith turned to Wyainalease, his voice heavy with curiosity. "Is there an alternative route?"

Wyainalease nodded, pressing her hands to her forehead, and began chanting.

A beam of luminescent green light emanated from her hands as she lowered them to reveal a gem.

Wyainalease deposited the gem into Slaith's hand. "With this, you and Loac will be safe."

Slaith glared at her as he spoke. "Why didn't you give us this in the first place?"

Wyainalease sighed, rolling her eyes in exasperation. "I hadn't expected you to be attacked. The forest creatures usually avoid humans."

Slaith grunted in response.

"There's one more thing you need," Wyainalease told him, disappearing into a different room before returning with a vial.

Wyainalease continued, "This is a potion. You will need this as Velinius has many monsters, especially Scanlists, lurking around her home. You must use this potion, as it will draw all the creatures to you. You need to run and hide as soon as it is released."

Slaith nodded, reaching out for the potion.

It slipped from his grasp, shattering against the floor and releasing a pungent scent of blood.

"What's in this?" Slaith inquired.

Wyainalease replied calmly, "Human blood mixed with Scanlist blood."

"I know that smell," Loac interrupted, his voice shaking, "it's the same smell from when the Scanlist attacked my father and me in the forest."

Loac's eyes darted towards Slaith. "Could it have been intentional? That it wasn't an accident that my home was attacked?"

Slaith returned the gaze, the weight of realisation sinking in. Slaith lowered his head, exhaling deeply.

"Yes, I think it was deliberate," Slaith confessed. "I encountered the same scent in a cottage in the village centre. It seems it was used to lead the Scanlist to your village."

Slaith paused, collecting his thoughts before continuing. "However, I still can't comprehend why your village was targeted. We will get our answers once we confront Velinius. And I fear whoever's pursuing us won't stop at anything until they get what they want. We need to find Velinius and end this."

Slaith turned to Loac; his expression changed to a sad one. "Do you think you will be strong enough for the journey? If we go, you must obey every word I say."

Loac nodded. "Yes, I will. I promise."

Slaith turned to Wyainalease. "What's your opinion? Will he be ready?"

Wyainalease chuckled darkly, "He'll be fit for travel after a night's rest, but whether he can withstand the dangers ahead is something we'll have to wait and see."

With that, Slaith settled beside Loac's bed, comforting Loac with a gentle smile. "For now, we rest. At first light, we will leave."

Loac's eyelids drooped, surrendering to sleep as Slaith retrieved his sword from a nearby table.

Seating himself on a stool, he glared at Wyainalease, who merely rolled her eyes, retreating to her room.

As morning dawned, Slaith and Loac prepared to depart.

Wyainalease intercepted Slaith.

Wyainalease spoke. "Velinius can only freeze you if she can see you for a few seconds, so listen to my warning. Make sure you are out of her sight and take this."

Wyainalease placed another bright orange gem in Slaith's hands, and Slaith looked at the gem.

Wyainalease spoke. "This gem is the only thing that will make her weak, and it must be placed on her; then you will attack her, but only have a few seconds, so make sure you act fast."

Slaith glanced at the gem, then back at Wyainalease, nodding.

Together, Slaith and Loac ventured into the shadowy forest until they spotted a large stone house barely visible, the soft glow of candlelight filtering through the branches.

Slaith crouched to meet Loac's gaze as he spoke. "This is the most dangerous situation we've faced. You must follow my instructions, no matter what. Do you understand?"

Loac gave a solemn nod. "I will listen."

Slaith gave a slight nod, surveying the forest before them.

They stood amidst a thick expanse of trees that blanketed their surroundings, offering a muted serenity disturbed only by the rustling of leaves.

Slaith straightened, his voice low but clear. "I believe this is the perfect spot to release the potions. As soon as I do, we run. You stay close, using the trees as cover. Based on what I know about the potion and that it didn't kill you or your father, it likely has a potent odour that the Scanlist is drawn to. So, we should be safe if we're not near the potion or directly in sight of the creatures."

With a sense of purpose, Slaith uncapped the bottle and spilt its contents onto the ground.

Slaith started running as he glanced back to see Loac following him as instructed.

A loud, screeching noise filled the air––the heavy thuds of paws hitting the ground as the creatures raced towards them.

Pale yellow eyes pierced the dim forest, seeking the alluring scent.

Slaith and Loac evaded the Scanlist by relying on their senses.

Eventually, the creature's screeches faded, and Slaith halted in front of a quaint stone house that resembled a miniature castle marred by scorch marks and chipped bricks.

Turning to Loac, Slaith instructed, "Please stay here and hide in that tree until I return."

Loac opened his mouth to protest, but Slaith's stern glare silenced him.

With a gulp, Loac nodded and climbed the tree as directed.

Slaith then turned to the house, inhaling deeply before venturing inside.

As he pushed the door open, it creaked gently, revealing a chilly, empty house.

It was built of stone, as cold as icicles in winter.

As Slaith moved deeper inside, candles flickered to life, casting long, eerie shadows that danced along the walls.

Slaith checked his pocket, confirming that the gem was there, and drew his sword from its sheath, cautiously navigating the frosty corridors.

Approaching a door with light seeping through its cracks, he heard the shuffle of feet against the stone floor.

Slaith slowly opened the door and peeked inside.

Velinius, the witch, was there, her back to him.

She was wearing a hooded cloak, adding herbs and earthy materials to a fire as she chanted.

Slaith scanned the room, large and shrouded in darkness except for a few areas illuminated by candles and surrounded by pillars.

But when Slaith stepped inside, a voice echoed, "So, you finally came. I was wondering when you and the boy would arrive."

Velinius' back was still turned, and she had a hood up, her black hair cascading from under it.

Remaining in the shadows, Slaith attempted to close the distance stealthily.

Slaith shouted from behind a pillar, "Why are you after me? Why did you poison my friend? Why did you attack Cruatan?"

"You are so simple-minded," Velinius cackled. "You honestly believed you were my main target? The boy is the one I seek."

As Slaith moved, the witch Velinius spun around, sending a flame in his direction.

Slaith evaded it and found cover behind another pillar.

Slaith called out, "Why are you after Loac?"

Velinius retorted, "Because my Master desires him. Now, enough talk. Come out of the shadows, and let's finish this."

Velinius raised her hands, ablaze with fire, her piercing green eyes and flowing black hair coming into view.

Velinius hurled flames in Slaith's direction, but he deftly rolled to safety and began slowly advancing on her.

Velinius grew frustrated, throwing flames around the room and letting out a scream that gradually filled the room with light as she began to breathe heavily.

Slaith seized the opportunity to charge in the sudden brightness, but she dodged his sword and sent him flying with a gust of wind.

As the room darkened again, Slaith retrieved his sword and began circling in the shadows, quietly closing in.

Suddenly, Velinius caught sight of Slaith and sent him sprawling with a massive push of her powers.

As Slaith fell, the gem tumbled from his pocket.

He heard its clattering sound as it struck the ground, then silence as it came to rest against something.

When Slaith tried to turn and locate the gem, he found himself paralysed, unable to move.

Slaith's heart started to race as he remained paralysed when he heard Loac's call, "Slaith!"

Velinius turned her gaze to Loac, cackling as she rushed past the frozen Slaith.

Velinius lifted Loac into the air, the atmosphere growing thick and heavy, just like when Loac was attacked earlier.

As Loac was lifted into the air, air rushed into his mouth as he gasped for breath.

Struggling and helpless, Loac found Velinius standing before him, a sinister grin on her face.

But when Loac looked back down, he saw Slaith limping, slowly advancing towards Velinius.

As soon as Slaith got near, Loac mustered all his strength to pass the gem to Slaith, who swiftly drove it into Velinius's back.

Velinius cried out in agony as Loac collapsed to the ground.

Seizing the opportunity, Slaith quickly grabbed his sword and plunged it into Velinius's back, demanding, "Tell me who your master is."

Velinius, coughing blood, attempted to laugh.

She hissed, "You know him, Slaith. You and the boy's parents both knew him."

Then, with a final, echoing laugh, Velinius died.

With her death, the room filled with light, and Wyainalease's voice echoed, "Thank you, I am now finally free."

The book Velinius had been using suddenly disappeared from the table.

Slaith scanned the room for any remnants of the two witches before rushing over to Loac, who slowly rose.

Loac smiled, asking, "What should we do now?"

Slaith sighed deeply, replying, "I don't know. I believe the threat is gone for now, but I don't know what to do next. I think it's time for us to visit Huvnor and his family to check their wellbeing. We should find somewhere safe to stay until we learn more about Velinius's master. But for now, we need to rest."

Loac nodded in agreement, and they both left, heading toward Huvnor and his family.

CHAPTER TWENTY
An Unsettling Home

Loac and Slaith finally arrived in Vastam and headed to the lodge in the village.

But before they could ask for a room, Lovila saw them both and waved at them excitedly.

"Hello! Slaith and Loac. What makes you both come by here? Do you need more jobs?"

Loac and Slaith walked toward Lovila.

Slaith's heart pounded when he saw her.

Slaith was about to speak, but Loac interrupted him. "We don't need any jobs. At the moment, we have somewhere else to be."

Slaith glared at Loac.

Loac looked around for Huvnor.

Lovila understood, so she quickly added, "Oh, I see you are looking for that family. I am happy to tell you they left shortly after you did. Your medicine helped Alluren greatly, and she was well enough to travel."

Slaith looked at Lovila with concern. "What do you mean by 'well enough'? Is she not fully healed?"

Lovila sighed. "I'm sorry. I don't think she will ever be fully healthy again."

Lovila continued, "She is walking and talking, but weak. However, she is alive, which wouldn't have been the case if you both hadn't helped."

Lovila smiled at Loac and said, "You did a good thing, Loac. You both saved her life."

Slaith asked, "Do you know where they went?"

Lovila nodded. "Yes, she told me they would return to their home."

Slaith's heart pounded as he became agitated. "What! I told them not to go back home. It's not safe."

Lovila's face lost its colour as she panicked. "I know, but Alluren isn't fully herself, and I advised them to stay somewhere familiar so she would be more comfortable and less anxious."

Slaith sighed. "Thank you. Anyway, we should go."

As Slaith and Loac turned to leave, Lovila smiled.

The sight of her smile caused Slaith's heart to race once again.

Lovila's soft voice filled Slaith's ears as she said, "Please visit when you are in town next. I would like to see both of you. Besides, I may have some interesting jobs for you."

Slaith returned the smile. "Of course. Thank you for all your help."

With that, they headed back to Huvnor and Alluren's hut.

They got to the hut where Huvnor and the family were staying, and the minute they jumped off Sage, Lily came running at them excitedly, embracing them. "Loac and Slaith are here! Loac and Slaith are here!"

Lily attempted to grab Loac's gear, but Loac took it first. "No, thank you, Lily, I can carry it myself."

Lily asked, "Please, can I carry something?"

Loac smiled and handed her a water bottle.

The little girl smiled and returned to the hut, holding the bottle.

Huvnor opened the door, smiled, and invited them in. "Come in. Alluren has just made food, and there is more than enough for you both, my friends."

Loac and Slaith smiled and spoke simultaneously. "How is she?"

As they walked through the door, Huvnor said with an ear-to-ear smile, "Well, you can see for yourself."

Alluren walked into the room slower than usual, looking more fragile but alive.

Slaith rushed to Alluren, hugged her, grabbed her by her shoulders, looked at her and asked, "How are you feeling?"

Alluren replied, "I am feeling fine. Well, weak, but fine. Thank you."

Alluren looked at Loac, who was next to Slaith. "I am alive because of you both, and I am very grateful."

Lily came in, bouncing with happiness. "Loac, Loac, can I show you the drawing that I made?"

Loac nodded, entered the room, and sat beside the fire.

Loac felt strange and uncomfortable, finding it hard to relax as he had been on the road for so long, but then Lily came over and showed the drawing.

Loac felt more at ease and smiled.

The drawing was of a young boy who looked like him, an older man who looked like Slaith with a sword, and the monster dead beside them.

Lily continued to show Loac her other drawings.

In the meantime, Slaith, Huvnor, and Alluren sat in the kitchen, and Slaith asked, "When you left the town, have you seen anything strange since?"

Alluren and Huvnor both shook their heads.

Loac overheard them talking and said to Lily, "I will return in a few minutes. Can you please draw a picture of something?"

Lily cheered, "Yes", with a smile.

Loac walked towards them and sat next to Slaith. "You sure you didn't notice anyone?"

Huvnor and Alluren both shook their heads.

Loac looked at Slaith, and Slaith asked again, "Did you hear anyone talking about Loac or myself before the attack or after?"

Alluren said, "No, we didn't even know you were in town. Never mind that you had the boy with you. Why are you asking?"

Slaith thought briefly before replying, "Well, the person who poisoned you said your family wasn't the target, nor was I. So, the only person left was Loac, but he is just a boy."

Looking at Loac, Slaith continued, "No offence, Loac. Do you have any idea why someone would be after you?"

Loac replied, "No, I don't. We lived in a quiet village. My mother and father kept to themselves except for a few people, and those people were like family. I only knew a few people, so I can't see why I was a target."

Slaith sighed. "Maybe they were after you because of me, but I don't know who and why, as I have angered many people. I was only around the boy for a short time."

Loac spoke. "Can we return to my hometown? Perhaps we'll uncover more clues there. After all that's happened, I'm convinced the attack wasn't accidental."

Slaith shook his head and responded angrily, "No, we are not returning to Cruatan. It's not safe. We'll find another way."

Loac countered, "We'll be okay. We've battled countless monsters already. If there's any lingering danger, we can handle it. I must understand why the village was attacked and why my parents were killed. Please, let's go."

Slaith rose to his feet, eyes boring into Loac's as he shouted, "I said no! It's not safe! We'll find another way, and that's final."

Loac, about to retaliate, was interrupted by Lily's heart-rending cries.

Both Slaith and Loac turned their attention to the distressed child.

With a resigned exhale, Loac conceded, "Alright, Slaith, have it your way," and approached Lily, trying to comfort her.

Slaith's gaze shifted to Huvnor, searching for understanding.

Huvnor remarked, "The boy has a point. You're likely safe enough to visit his home. If the threats are gone, you could discover more about the attack, and Loac's suspicions are correct. Why won't you consider Cruatan?"

Slaith sighed heavily. "Cruatan now is a haunting reminder of all Loac once held dear. He's still so young, and I don't believe he's fully come to terms with the death of his parents. Seeing Cruatan in its current state might traumatise him further. He's not ready. We'll search elsewhere for now. If we find nothing, I might reconsider returning to Cruatan when he's older and more prepared—only when I deem it right, not just when he feels ready, unless..."

Slaith paused, gathering his thoughts. "He truly comprehends the weight of what he might witness. I fear the sight of Cruatan in its present state might be too devastating."

Huvnor nodded, understanding the depth of Slaith's concerns.

There was silence for a few minutes, and Alluren called Lily and Loac over, and they sat down at dinner, eating and laughing and enjoying each other's company.

Alluren eventually put her daughter to bed and said, "Loac, I have your bed ready whenever you want to sleep."

Loac said, "Thank you. I will go to sleep in a while."

Together, they talked and laughed into the night.

In the morning, Loac and Slaith gathered the gear, said their goodbyes to the family and headed to the town called Liberanit.

It took about two days to get there, and it was a small town like Cruatan.

The people were very welcoming to the strangers.

They walked to a lodge.

At the reception, the man asked them grumpily, "What do you want?"

Slaith smirked. "Is that how you treat an old friend?"

A short man, barely reaching five feet in height, perched his round glasses on his nose, squinting through them.

The man looked up and smiled. "Oh! It's you, Slaith. I apologise for my tone. I just had little kids playing tricks on me all day, so I am not in the best form."

He continued, "Anyway, what made you come here? Is it to see an old friend?"

"Not exactly. I want to stay here for a while with Loac." Slaith turned to look at Loac.

"Oh!" the man said. "I didn't know you had a child."

Slaith corrected him. "No, he isn't mine, but I look after him. So, I wonder if you can find us a place to stay, and I will pay as soon as I earn more coins."

The man waved his hand. "Yes, of course. I will find you the finest place, which is yours for free if you need it."

"No, there is no need." Slaith felt a bit uncomfortable.

The man seemed adamant. "I insist, and that is it."

Slaith replied, "Thanks."

The man directed them to where they would live.

It was like a mini cottage. Upon entering the house, they were greeted by a cosy sitting area with soft cushions and a plush couch that faced a small fireplace.

The fireplace was surrounded by stones and logs, giving the room a warm and inviting feel.

The sitting area was connected to a small kitchen with a wooden dining table, chairs, and the essential kitchenware needed to prepare meals.

Two bedrooms were at the far end of the cottage, separated by a small hallway.

Each bedroom had a comfortable bed with soft pillows and blankets, a wardrobe for clothes, and a window that allowed natural light to filter in.

Loac ran, jumped on his bed, and sighed with relief that he finally would sleep on this comfortable bed for a long time, as opposed to the uncomfortable ground that always had a foul smell because of Sage.

Slaith walked into the room and smiled when he saw Loac's happiness.

Then Slaith went to his room to wash up, but kept looking around him and thinking restlessly about where he would go next.

But then, he remembered that this was his new home for now.

Slaith felt lost and out of place as he unpacked his belongings and placed them in a room that was his for the first time in years.

It felt bizarre and unnerving to him.

Slaith looked outside through the window into the forest.

All he wanted to do was pack up his things and live on the road again, but then he thought about Loac and sighed.

He grunted to himself and finished unpacking.

Once he finished unpacking his gear, Loac came rushing in, excited. "How do you like your room?"

Slaith replied, "It is okay."

Loac grinned. "Well, sleeping next to Sage on the ground isn't better. He stinks, after all."

Slaith let out a little chuckle as he spoke. "I got quite used to that. This place feels unusual to me."

Loac said in a sadder voice, "Oh really, I am..." but Slaith interrupted before Loac could finish his sentence, knowing he would apologise and probably even suggest they leave.

"Never mind, Loac. I know that I will love this place in time. So, let's go and see what this town offers us."

Slaith grabbed his sword and put it on his back, and Loac was ready to leave, but saw Slaith wearing his sword and said, "Do you think you will need that anymore?"

Slaith turned and looked at the sword.

Slaith's heart sank, and he let out a deep sigh.

"You make a valid point, Loac," Slaith admitted. "I've worn this sword out of habit, and while it may no longer serve a practical purpose, it holds a special significance for me. It's a source of comfort and a connection to my past. I'll continue to carry it."

Loac nodded with a smile, and they left the room to look around the town.

The town was lively; the people were happy, and there was no tension.

Loac's belly rumbled, and he looked at Slaith, smiled, and made a small laugh. "I suppose we know where we are going next."

They walked around the stall to see any tasty food that caught their eyes.

Slaith kept looking for food that he was familiar with, but there was so much variety and different food combinations that he needed help finding something to eat.

Eventually, Loac smelled something very familiar, like the bread that Margaret (the baker in Cruatan) used to make.

Loac started to run towards the smell and eventually reached the stall, where there was a female baker with her back turned.

Loac said, "Excuse me," in a cheery tone.

The baker turned around, and Loac's heart sank when he saw that the woman wasn't Margaret.

The woman asked cheerfully, "Is there anything I can get you?"

Loac didn't respond and kept looking at the ground, lost for words.

Slaith followed and saw Loac and the lady looking concerned. "Yes, can you please get us two cups of soup and a loaf of bread?"

The woman looked at Slaith. "No problem," she said.

Slaith stood next to Loac and grabbed him by the side. "Are you okay?"

Loac looked at Slaith with a fake smile. "Yes, I am fine. Just thought she was someone I recognised..."

The woman came back with the food, and they walked away.

Loac kept looking around the place.

The vibrant town made him happy and sad, bringing back memories of his hometown before the troubles happened.

Slaith could read Loac's mood, and he asked, "How do you feel about this town so far?"

Loac replied, "I like it so far. It feels strange and familiar at the same time. I keep getting the feeling that I know these people. However, they are strangers to us. It is so strange. I am unsure how I feel, but I already feel like this place is my home, and I can't wait to get to know the people."

Loac waited a second and then asked, "What about you, Slaith?"

Slaith replied, "I feel the same way."

It was a white lie because what was familiar to Slaith was being on the road with Sage, fighting creatures, visiting Huvnor and Alluren, and now spending time with Loac. Everything else felt foreign and strange.

They kept looking through the shops and talking to people briefly until Slaith retreated to the room, unable to bear talking to another person.

Loac stayed in the town and kept looking around.

Loac returned to Slaith's room.

Sitting on Slaith's bed, Loac said, "I feel comfortable with this town. It seems closer to my hometown than the other villages we visited. Do you think we will stay here, Slaith, for a while, anyway?"

Slaith looked at Loac and saw how happy and relaxed he was.

Slaith nodded. "I knew you would feel like that. That is why I picked this place. I will like this place in time. I need to get used to it, but of course, we will stay here as long as you like."

As they both looked outside the window into the vibrant town, Slaith started to think again about why Loac was attacked. Will they come and find Loac again to finish the job?

Slaith then looked at Loac and knew he would protect him at all costs.

Loac then looked back at Slaith and hugged him impulsively as he stared at the window.

Slaith then began to feel a sense of calm and belonging wash over him.

Slaith realised he had found a new home, not just in this town, but with Loac.

The road had been his life for so long, but now he saw more to life than just travelling and seeking adventure.

He had found a new purpose in looking after Loac.

Slaith spoke to Loac with a small smile and said, "I think we can make a life here, at least for a while."

Loac beamed with happiness and nodded in agreement as they stared out the window at the town.